THE SCRIBE
AND THE LOTUS

THE SCRIBE
AND THE LOTUS

BAKR FAHMY

authorHOUSE®

AuthorHouse™
1663 Liberty Drive
Bloomington, IN 47403
www.authorhouse.com
Phone: 1-800-839-8640

Published by AuthorHouse   11/08/2012

ISBN: 978-1-4772-4288-9 (sc)
ISBN: 978-1-4772-4289-6 (e)

Contents

Part 1 : **Peret** (The coming forth of the land out of the inundation.)

Part 2 : **Shemu** (The Harvest)

Part 3 : Akhet (The Flood)

To the Children of Egypt who dared to stand up and let their voices be heard across the world.

Corruption, what corruption?
How do you fight
Corruption
In the hearts?
Stay pure
Think of the lotus
As it blooms
In the morning light
A beacon of fire
In the dark night
Hold your course
Helmsman
Even though you must
Throw out
The excess ballast
To steady your bark.

Bakr M. Fahmy
Sakkara, 2011

Foreword

At the height of its glory, Men-nefer (Memphis) was one of the largest cities of the ancient world. Its splendors included massive temples, palaces and houses, all enclosed by the city's legendary "White Walls."

Its harbour was crowded with ships from far-off lands, laden with exotic, imported goods, such as cedar wood, patterned cloth and rare metals. The city's business was carried out in countless open-air markets, offices and workshops.

At the heart of Memphis was its chief temple complex, an immense sprawl of shrines, statues and gateways, all dedicated to the creator god Ptah and his family, Sekhmet and Nefertum.

Religion permeated every aspect of life in the ancient city. Men and women at all levels of society worshipped privately in their homes, and appealed for divine assistance through devotional images and amulets worn on their bodies.

Animals sacred to various gods, such as the ibis and other birds, baboons, crocodiles and massive bulls, to name a few, lived pampered lives in special tended areas.

These animals, which were considered to contain within them the essence of divine power, were also seen as living representatives of the gods.

Like humans, sacred animals were often mummified and buried in the city of the dead, lying further west in the great cemeteries of Saqqara.

But in Egypt during the reign of Qakare Ibi[1], in the years 2169-2167 B.C., the country had been divided into at least three parts. The Old Kingdom had finally come to an end and a new era of uncertainty had been born.

The so-called 'First Intermediate' period was *not* a "Dark Age." The calamity triggered by low Nile floods was the impetus to radical social changes and a reformulation of the notion of kingship. The legacy of this period is still with us today.

*   *   *

---

[1]   His existence was established by the discovery of his small pyramid in South Saqqara which also continues the late Old Kingdom tradition of listing pyramid texts in his tomb. His name is mentioned in both line 53 of the Abydos King List and by the Turin Canon. The Turin Canon assigns him a short reign lasting "2 years, 1 month and 1 day".

Chapter 1

Carrying the sun, Khepri, the black scarab takes its painful first step into the scintillating light of dawn, a shiny glimmer of reddish orange that blinds the eye. The canal's late night silence lays down its head, surrendering to the last sore groans of a bullfrog and the buzz of a fly, angrily fighting for its first meal.

The nearby water's lotus petals begin to open and the fragrance of a new day engulfs the swampy scents of the passing night.

No more darkness: to the ground, your mourning shroud.

Hearing the shrill and eerie call of the Senegal Thick-knee, *"ee, ee,* ee, eee" Thut-nefer, a tall and slender young man awakens to the glory of another Egyptian sunrise breaking through the open doorway of his small mud hut.

For all those who have a heart to see, it's not actually the eyes that go blind, but the heart, he muses, opening his eyes wide.

Thut-nefer runs his hand across his shaven head. Irritated by the stubble he kicks aside the linen sheet and slowly gets up. Taking a deep breath he steps through the narrow door.

The cool morning breeze plays on his cheeks, as he looks up at the sky inquisitively. "Another hot day ahead, with not a cloud in sight," he murmurs to himself. "Better get a move on."

Thut-nefer grabs his handmade net from its hanging place on the side of the hut. For a moment, he feels the strength of it between his fingers, woven of palm tree fibre, and thinks of his friend, Nar, who had painstakingly made it for him, specifically to suit his throw.

Pausing to adjust his sandals, he glances back proudly at the mud hut he'd built for himself from the dense black soil of the Nile. He recalls with a smile the back-breaking hours he had spent, making and building the sun-dried bricks.

Here, Thut-nefer would stow away his catch of the sacred Ibis and enjoy his few precious moments of solitude, away from his work and studies.

Intertwining itself along the crude sun shelter made of broken branches, and reaching for the roof of the mud hut, the flowering grape vine he had planted for shade blossoms brightly with a promise of the grapes to come.

Setting off, in search of Nar, Thut-nefer gently pats his dark grey donkey on the head, as it lazily chews on some leftovers from its evening feed. Playfully he pulls at one of its ears. The donkey snorts and stomps its front hoof in firm acknowledgement, happy with its master's attention. He mimics a snort and laughs contentedly.

"Wait for me here, and don't wander off, my loyal friend. I'll be back to get you soon."

While Thut-nefer knows that in a few hours, Khentiki, his master tutor, and the rest of his fellow classmates will start missing him at scribe school, it doesn't bother him in the least; for he has chosen this day to spend some time outside in solitude; and in doing so, by basking in the embrace of nature, he trusts he'll feel back in his element.

The first rays of the sun glitter off the top of King Djoser's pyramid, majestically positioned high above the sea of palm trees, as if they were locking up an ancient portal to the underworld. Thut-nefer cannot help but gasp at the sight, even though he's seen it a thousand times.

As a fly lands on his brow, he brushes it aside with a quick motion of his hand.

Imhotep, master of masters, here I am looking up at your achievements, from mud to stone and from stone to mud, he muses, dropping his net.

Thut-nefer picks up a handful of moist black earth, and takes in a deep breath. Inhaling its raw, dark scent sends a tingling sensation down his spine, as if infusing him with a new vitality.

Lifting his head to the already blazing sun ascending in the morning sky, he whispers aloud, "O Atum, creator of the great Nile, giver of all life . . ." then sighs, "Who am I to complain?"

Dropping the handful of mud into the irrigation ditch, he bends over, picks up his net, and sets off at a brisk pace towards the column of smoke lazily floating in the nearly windless sky.

*   *   *

Nar's round face gleams with pleasure, and his eyes, black as the Egyptian night, sparkle with a fiery intensity at the sight of his approaching friend.

Thut-nefer stops in midstride, looking over his friend's garb: a coarse linen kilt, sloppily tied around his waist, reed sandals covered in black mud, with one hardened hand grasping his flint knife, the other waving a half-cleaned fish.

"Greetings, my fisherman friend," Thut-nefer calls out.

"Greetings, o' Scribe," Nar retorts, with a slight hint of sarcasm in his voice. "Your presence illuminates my humble fireplace. Be seated and I'll make you breakfast."

Thut-nefer approaches and sits down on a reed mat next to the open-air fire. Three medium-sized tilapia each one skewered onto a palm branch, cook on the embers of Nar's fire.

"How are you?" asks Thut-nefer. "Has the great God been generous to you?"

"Yes and no," Nar murmurs back, somewhat agitated as he looks around for a piece of palm bark to wipe clean the clay plate in his hand.

"I only caught four tilapias, a couple of small catfish, and a large eel, which I've wrapped up and put in that basket for you to take home for your mother."

"Really, Nar, you're the truth that makes alive! And so is my stomach going to live through the truth of hunger pangs, if you're not going to bring that breakfast now!"

Nar deftly grabs the palm branches with the fish, and lays them gently onto the plate. He reaches over for his pouch, unties the knot, and retrieves a large loaf of bread, an onion, a ripe lemon, and a small bundle of cloth.

While he carefully unties the cloth with both hands, the scent of mixed festival spices wafts through the fresh morning air.

Nar gently pulls at the dorsal bone of a tilapia and eases out the sharp, spiny bones from the succulent white flesh. He picks up a lemon and takes a small bite, exposing the white interior.

Wincing at its tang, he squeezes carefully, allowing a few drops of lemon juice to drip onto the fish. That done, he crushes the onion with the palm of his hand, and decides to split it into four.

Lightly sprinkling the steaming fish with the precious festival spice, he tenderly lays it on a piece of bread. Thut-nefer, watching Nar's surgically precise actions with great interest, thankfully accepts the deboned fish.

The two men, now comfortably sitting cross-legged and face-to-face, begin to silently devour the food before them.

With the tilapia quickly disappearing from the plate, Nar begins mopping up the last of the fish on a morsel of bread. He dips it into the spices, and pops it gently into his mouth, slowly chewing the last scrap with great delight.

"I sold the three ibis mummies yesterday to the pilgrims," Nar casually relays.

Looking over at his silent friend, Nar asks, "Are you going to hunt ibis today?"

He offers an earthenware jug of water to Thut-nefer, who takes hold of it with both hands and drinks slowly, enjoying the naturally cooled water. He hands it back with a grateful nod.

"They're getting harder to sell, you know," Nar warns. "I meant to tell you, but I see you have a lot of things on your mind these days. What's bothering you, anyway? One moment you're here, and the next you're drifting on my papyrus boat through the reed marshes amongst the ducks!"

Thut-nefer prefers to remain silent, saying nothing. Instead, he looks straight up into the sky.

"And you know why they're harder to sell," Nar continues persistently, "because of this- . . . *this.*"

Again he leans over and brusquely reaches for another larger basket, where he keeps his catch.

Solemnly, he sits up. As if by magic, Nar produces a large bundle, unravels the coarse linen cloth, and reveals a beautifully painted mummy of a sacred ibis.

He drops it next to Thut-nefer. In one swift motion, Nar crushes it with his fist, rams his crude flint knife into it, and exposes the insides, as if he is disemboweling a freshly caught fish.

Staring at it with disgust, he let's fly a curse under his breath. Only a few jumbled words reach Thut-nefer's ears, while he tentatively bends over to examine the ruptured mummy.

"It's a fake," Thut-nefer declares, wide-eyed, yet unimpressed. "I could see that right away. There's nothing but a feather, a broken bone, and a palm branch."

He glares straight into Nar's eyes, who returns the look with a glint in his own eyes.

Thut-nefer, catching on to his friend's drift, announces curtly, "I won't revert to these kind of abominations!"

"It's cheaper to make, and we can get more for them," Nar replies offhandedly, trying to appeal to Thut-nefer's common sense.

"Bend with the wind, as the reeds do."

Displeasure, tainted with disgust, creeps across Thut-nefer's face.

"I won't do it, and that's final! I've got four more mummies to wrap and that'll be the end of my supply of ingredients."

Sensing Thut-nefer's displeasure, Nar shrugs his shoulders, deciding not to pursue the matter any further. He hastily adds, "We've got two large vessels of festival spice I traded the mummies for, from the people of the oasis. Seeing it's harvest season soon, we should store them until then."

"Good . . . good. I'm not going to hunt ibis today. If you help me, we can finish wrapping those four mummies and you can take them with you. I'm going to be busy in the coming days with the cattle count. My mother has sent you some date cakes, so you'd better collect them now."

"Your mother is the truth that makes alive," Nar blurts out. "May the great God bless her with ankh, seneb and udja!"

Thut-nefer interrupts him quickly before he can begin one of his typically lengthy monologues of gratitude and praise.

"Let's go, fisherman!" he barks out impatiently, moving out back toward his mud hut, unwilling to wait for Nar.

*   *   *

Gently strolling up to his donkey, Thut-nefer unties the palm bark rope from around its front legs, and gives it an affectionate scratch on the nose. The donkey, sensing its master's will, acknowledges it with a short snort, then trots over to the irrigation ditch to drink.

Nar scrapes through the ashes of the previous night's fire, hoping to find an ember to rekindle it again.

Thut-nefer steps into the mud hut and pauses for a moment, allowing his eyes to acclimate. Standing in the rudimentary workspace he'd spent countless hours in before, he takes in the familiar surroundings: the sweet scent of the myrrh and frankincense resin, a stone slab, three large jars, and a number of reed baskets of different size and shape.

Four birds lay on the stone slab, ready to be embalmed. The linen had been cut into strips of one cubit in length, and lay in a basket on the ground.

Everything's ready, now, for the final step in the embalming process, Thut-nefer affirms to himself.

He checks the jars filled with frankincense and myrrh, and then the one full of natron salt, while waiting for Nar to bring the clay incense burner he was loading with hot coals.

Nar steps into the doorway, temporarily blocking the sunlight from outside and casting a shadow over the stone slab. He reaches over and hands the burner to Thut-nefer, who carefully places it next to the stone.

"Get the incense balls from the small basket, put some on the coals, and sprinkle the ground with water and natron," he orders.

Nar solemnly obeys. Thut-nefer sits down cross-legged in front of the stone slab, and fishes out a rolled up papyrus scroll from amongst his things.

He slowly unrolls the papyrus, waiting for Nar to finish sprinkling the ground with water. The incense smoke begins to unfurl itself in wispy plumes in the rays of light coming through the door. Soon, the room is enveloped in a thick, aromatic cloud.

Thut-nefer takes a deep breath of the sweet scent and begins to read aloud, steady and rhythmic, almost melodious.

"A voice is raised in the northern sky, and wailing is heard in the marsh land, because of the voice summoning the blessed one.

I am raised up to the place where Ma 'at is. I have flown up to them as a swallow, like Thoth; I cackle to them as a goose.[2]"

He repeats, again and again, the same verse, until he breaks into a chant. Nar stands behind Thut-nefer, mesmerized by the words, unable to move.

His eyes shine with excitement, mirroring the incredible love in his heart for this young scribe's chanting. Suddenly, Thut-nefer falls silent. Nothing moves, but the incense smoke dancing in the rays of the sun. Slowly, it winds its way down and out, being sucked through the opening at the base of the door—liberated at last, it vanishes and becomes one with the outside world.

The hut begins to clear of the smoky incense, and Thut-nefer begins to read again:

"I am he who rises and lights up wall after wall, each thing in succession. There will not be a day that lacks its owed illumination. Pass on, o' creatures, pass on, o' world! Listen!

---

[2]   Spell 205. Egyptian Book of the Dead

I have ordered you to! I am the cosmic blue lotus that rose shining from Nun's black primordial waters, and my mother is Nut, the night sky!

O, you who made me, I have arrived! I am the great ruler of yesterday! The power of command is in my hand![3]"

Thut-nefer ties the final knot on the last ibis. He closes his eyes for a moment to relieve the strain, slowly reopens them, and lovingly looks at his work. He slowly nods in satisfaction.

Nar, catching the cue, hands him two small pots of ready mixed pigments, each with its own reed pen. With a steady hand, Thut-nefer paints in eyes, beak and some feathers.

"How's that?" he half murmurs to himself. Now, don't move them until they're dry, Nar."

"You have improved greatly, o' Sesh! You are a real master! Your hand is straight and your heart pure." He pauses and turns his head toward the door.

"I think I hear somebody coming- . . ."

Not waiting to finish the sentence Nar nervously leaps through the small doorway, leaving Thut-nefer to pack away all the tools. Outside he hears two voices talking excitedly, and then a burst of laughter.

"It's my sister, Meryt-mi-hapi," Nar calls from outside. "She wishes to greet you, o' Sesh. She has brought my midday meal."

Thut-nefer, relieved, steps out through the door, slightly stooping, so as not to bump his head. Once outside, he straightens himself, and looks at the sun high up in the cloudless sky, realizing that he has spent most of the morning in his mud hut.

Meryt-mi-hapi approaches shyly, wearing a dress made of coarse linen. She is bare footed, and carefully balancing a wicker basket full of lotus flowers on her head.

---

[3]   Spell 42, The Book of the Dead

Around her neck dangles a necklace made of turquoise faience, matching the brilliant colour of the Egyptian sky. In deep contrast, her big black eyes, carefully made-up with kohl, shine like finely polished basalt.

"Greetings, o' Sesh," she chirps gaily, happy to see him. Her brother helps her lower the basket to the ground, as he hurriedly rummages through the contents and fishes out his lunch bundle.

She grabs it from him, walks over to a shady spot under the lone palm tree and starts to prepare the meal of salted dried fish, cucumbers and bread.

"Your mother, o' Sesh, kindly took me to the House of Life[4] yesterday before sunset," Mery-mi-hapi comments haphazardly while watching the men eat, "and she begs you to come home immediately."

"Oh, yes," Thut-nefer manages to reply between mouthfuls, "and why did you go to the House of Life?"

"All girls my age have an amulet necklace to keep the evil eye away!" Meryt-mi-hapi counters evasively, her gaze carefully lowered. She raises both hands and strokes her turquoise necklace lovingly.

Nar coughs sarcastically and puts a mock grimace across his face.

Laughing heartily, he blurts out, "Really, Meryt, you expect us to believe that! More like you're looking to open up a house."

Meryt-mi-hapi gives her brother a piercing look, her black eyes digging deep into her brother's, causing him to fall silent.

---

4   The House of Life, an ancient healing center, is run by priests who provide prescriptive cures for common ills, interpret dreams, and supply magical spells, charms and incantations of various kinds.

"My brother doesn't understand," she complains reproachfully, standing her ground. "You see, here . . ."

Thut-nefer looks up at the young girl, shyly twirling between her thumb and forefinger, a necklace composed of multi-colored faience beads, interspersed with seven blue carved faience amulets, each representing a deity.

"And so . . . you were given something to add to your already bountiful beauty." Thut-nefer quietly gasps, as he sees the young girl blush, her cheeks turning into the color of a fine carnelian stone.

"What did you learn about each of those stones?" he adds quickly, hoping to allow her to regain her composure.

Picking one up from the rest, she replies coolly, "This one depicts Isis, wearing the solar horned disc crown and nursing Horus as a child."

Holding the stone next to it, she continues, "Bastet, daughter of the sun god, represented as a benevolent cat goddess. Then, there's Nefertum, god of the primeval lotus blossom, the image of perfection, followed by Ptah, the creator god of Memphis."

Meryt-mi-hapi gazes for a moment into the eyes of her brother's friend, eliciting an affectionate smile from him. She continues, "Sekhmet, the lioness, who can both cause and cure diseases, is on this stone."

She fingers yet another of the stones on her necklace.

"Thoth, the baboon, the god who inspires wisdom, is symbolized by this one, and Taweret, the hippopotamus, goddess of fertility, is this one. She protects everyone involved in childbirth."

Letting go of the necklace, she looks to see how both men are responding to her description.

"Good, Meryt-mi-hapi, good," Thut-nefer encourages her, delighted by the young girl's awareness. "That's a very powerful combination. I truly hope it keeps the evil away from your path."

A hedgehog scuttles out from behind the mud hut, and darts between the donkey's legs, straight for the nearest bush. The donkey, indignant, snorts loudly, and they all break out laughing.

"You see, Meryt-mi-hapi, you are blessed!" Thut-nefer guffaws, acknowledging the hilarity of the situation.

Turning to Nar, Thut-nefer smiles and continues, "I have further errands to do before nightfall, so must bid you both farewell. It was good to spend some time with you!" Both his friends nod and give Thut-nefer a heartfelt embrace.

"I, too, must finish several tasks," answers Nar, "and so I say good-bye to you, as well, o' Sesh."

Within moments, the two siblings disappear behind a row of castor oil trees growing along the canal.

*　　*　　*

Chapter 2

In the faint distance, Thut-nefer hears the song of a lonely shepherd, coming from the direction of an old pockmarked fig sycamore he'd climbed as a child.

"It's time to return to the human swamp," he calls out to the donkey and bends over to retrieve two lotus flowers that had fallen out of Meryt-mi-hapi's basket.

The scent of the blue lotus overpowers his senses, and sends his emotions reeling.

"Mer," he whispers . . . "love." He lets his mind draw the hoe, the hieroglyphic sign for love, in his best possible script.

Yes, he thinks to himself, *I must pass by the fig sycamore and say a prayer.*

"Back to the human swamp!" he calls out again, this time to the universe while taking a deep breath of the blossom.

He enters the hut and collects all his belongings, hurriedly throwing them into the two baskets that make up the donkey's rig.

Above the doorway, just below the palm trunk beam, Thut-nefer notices, for the first time, a small, circular crack in the mud plaster. He picks up his walking staff and knocks lightly on the wall, until the mud plaster falls away, revealing a small round hole, just big enough to fit a large fist.

Slowly inserting his hand, he feels the thin edges of something familiar. Opening his hand wider and reaching further back into the hole, he grasps the object and begins pulling it out. As he gets it in front of his eyes, he sees he has retrieved a papyrus scroll. He dusts it carefully using the bottom of his kilt.

Sitting down cross-legged on the ground, Thut-nefer unrolls the scroll and begins to read, his lips silently twitching in anticipation.

"A title deed! Great Atum! You reveal what is hidden!" he exclaims out loud and reads on. "A title deed, issued to Neferefre—my *father*—for a parcel of property in the nome of Men-nefer.[5] And, it's officially approved with the King's seal!."

The governor must have confiscated the entire property when Father died without having the title deed in his possession. Even the swine-herders have more pride than this thief who calls himself governor, he contemplates excitedly.

Thut-nefer's mind reels with wild thoughts about what he has just discovered.

Nefer knew of this place, and what's more, he must have actually come here and hid this deed under their very noses.

"O Neferefre," he exclaims, looking up at the neat row of palm branches that make up the ceiling of the mud hut, "scribe of the palace of the King of Men-nefer. A great injustice has been committed after your death, and yet you foresaw the evil and managed to hide this title deed away from your enemies in this unobtrusive mud hut."

Thut-nefer quietly chuckles to himself, lowering his gaze.

The beak of the ibis is the finger of the scribe. Take care not to distress it, he muses. *Yes, indeed, these old proverbs ring so true.*

---

[5]   Memphis

The scribe's mind is as sharp as the ibis's beak and can draw blood, especially when it's being provoked.

He laughs out loud, surprised at what he has just stated aloud.

I must hide this, back into the hole under the palm trunk beam. O' Great One, men salute thee.

Thut-nefer nervously returns the scroll back to its secret resting place. Once done and satisfied the precious scroll has been concealed properly, he steps outside and pulls at the rope around the donkey's neck, wishing to quickly get a move on.

His pensive mood, though, hinders him from a quick getaway, as he fumbles about, collecting his thoughts.

The song of the shepherd, now rising louder, penetrates Thut-nefer's subconscious, as he walks, still deep in thought, along the path to the southern sycamore.

On both sides of the path, the emmer wheat, almost ripe, glitters in the late afternoon sunshine. A sense of excitement at the approaching harvest adds a light spring to his walk.

He hastily makes his way towards the majestic fig sycamore, where both man and beast seek her soothing shade.

"Greetings, O Sesh," lisps the old lead herdsman, casually leaning on his staff. His face, raw and parched, like a well-dried sheet of papyrus, is deeply tanned from continual exposure to the merciless Egyptian sun.

The old man's toothless grin, also, stands out to Thut-nefer, reminding him of his humble roots as a child, herding his own family's beasts.

Thut-nefer takes an immediate liking to this simple man.

"You humble us with your presence, o' Sesh. Rest your weary limbs . . ." He points to the mat and the water jug.

Thut-nefer decides to accept this man's hospitality, leaving his donkey to the small boy, who suddenly appears from nowhere.

"Greetings, herdsman. What beautiful animals you slaughter."

"The Great One has been most generous this year," lisps the headman, looking up at the topmost branches of the sycamore, to evade Thut-nefer's inquisitive stare.

"What? You slaughter your best animals before the King's cattle count? You know better! No slaughter should be done until the count has been declared, otherwise how are we going to know the exact numbers of all the animals!"

"The Governor of Men-nefer has sent for six of my best animals, to be brought to him before night fall," the headman interrupts quickly realizing the young man before him could be a scribe and therefore easily aroused to suspicion.

He finally looks Thut-nefer in the eyes and moans, "My herd . . . my herd!"

The man does not have to continue, for Thut-nefer reads the sadness and the pain in his eyes only too well; and yet, he also detects a glint of indomitable fury towards the injustice being foisted upon him, an upright man.

"Heb . . . to persevere" Thut-nefer whispers, letting his fluid mind draw the hieroglyphic symbol of an ibis.

"Let it be known that, indeed, men are like ibises. Squalor is throughout the land, and there are none whose clothes are white in these times. So be brave, noble herdsman, and stand your ground. Heb!"

Thut-nefer's eyes wander over to the two carcasses hanging on the lowest branches of the sycamore. A man stands beneath them, skilfully gutting the animals, removing their entrails, which drop to the ground and are quickly retrieved by a young boy.

"Say your prayer, o Scribe," rasps the old herdsman, now gazing straight and deep into Thut-nefer's eyes "under this blessed tree. Let it come from deep inside your heart, like a young calf calling for its mother.

See, I have placed you on the path of God. The fate of a man is placed on his shoulders on the day he is born. Now go, before anyone sees you congregating with common cattle poachers. In these times, even honest men are turned into thieves."

The old herdsman nudges his head, and the young boy disappears, only to re-appear a few moments later with the scribe's donkey. Taking hold of the rope around the beast's neck Thut-nefer fishes out his last jug of beer and sets it down on the mat.

"Greetings, my herdsman!" Thut-nefer answers, gazing at the headman. "The blow that doesn't break your back will only strengthen you."

"Greetings, o' Scribe! You are a good man! May God bless you with ankh, udja and seneb."

Thut-nefer regretfully leaves the shade of the lady of the sycamore and plunges into the intense afternoon sun.

He walks in silence for some time, allowing his thoughts to settle down and his mind to become more still. He watches an unkempt toddler being led by a very large cow proudly carrying its vast horns.

The boy, distracted by a pair of hoopoe skirmishing over a morsel of bread, drops his sling, stumbles and falls.

He lets go of the handmade rope tied to the cow's ear. Having lost its protégé, the cow instinctively slows down to wait for the rope to go taut again. The boy, quickly retrieves his sling, grabs hold of the rope and they both gather their rhythmic momentum once more.

Thut-nefer chuckles to himself and intuitively strokes his donkey's mane . . . *What a beautiful and caring beast. I wonder who is taking care of whom? Are we taking care of our animals or are they taking care of us? That's a good question,* he muses.

Abruptly, the dusty path along the irrigation ditch comes to an end. Thut-nefer turns left and follows a larger canal that leads to the outskirts of Men-nefer. Further down, along the canal, he makes out a group of people causing a furor.

Too far to hear precisely what the raised angry voices are saying, still, he sees men with their wooden hoes pointing towards the canal and waving their arms above their heads.

Not paying attention to the uneven path, Thut-nefer's left foot slips out of his rush and papyrus sandal, causing him to stumble. He stops momentarily, slides his foot back into the sandal and looks up, just barely recognizing the figure of a man, a stone's throw away, standing shoulder deep in the brown waters of the canal.

"That man works for my neighbor! He's the assistant supervisor," he comments to no one in particular.

Slowly, Thut-nefer starts walking again. His donkey eagerly nudges him in his back and the master naturally picks up the pace. Within moments, Thut-nefer approaches close enough to hear the tirade of insults being hurled.

"The evil-doer, throw him in the canal, and he will bring back its slime!" shouts a short stout man, brandishing his wooden hoe high above his head.

"The members of your family ought to be gathered together and be made to summon a crocodile!" bellows another, this time directly at the figure standing in the water.

A chorus of approval breaks out among the crowd. Sensing potential danger *and* home, and not wanting to break its pace, the donkey nudges Thut-nefer in the back once again. Firmly tugging at the rope around its neck, he slows down for a moment to catch a glimpse of the culprit.

Back in the swamp, Thut-nefer thinks to himself. *O' Atum, give us the strength and knowledge needed to trudge through this quagmire. This man must have rerouted an irrigation ditch, hoping to appropriate more water.*

He thinks of Meryt-mi-hapi and her basket full of blue lotuses, then smiles, wiping the perspiration off his brow with his fore finger.

Thut-nefer wipes his hand on his linen kilt and strokes the ptah amulet dangling around his neck, given to him by Khentika, the master scribe, his teacher and mentor.

"Live by the truth and the truth will live by you!" he mutters to himself.

Isn't that what he always said? Yes, indeed, a wise old man, drowning in the muddy swamp with no one to hear him out, already forgotten and not even dead.

The truth that comes alive! Raise your head high, close your mouth to trap your tongue, and then enter the White Wall[6], o' Scribe.

Thut-nefer could tell he was getting closer to home now; the path was getting wider and smoother. Stall after stall, selling a variety of goods and vegetables, lines both sides of the lane. Four women carrying fully loaded wicker baskets precariously balanced on their heads block his path.

"Make way!" Thut-nefer shouts at them over the din of the stall vendors. They move slowly under the heavy burden, causing the man behind Thut-nefer to lose patience.

"Move, women!" he yells indignantly, as he hustles past, brandishing his staff menacingly. Thut-nefer ignores him, looking for the turn-off that would lead him towards his family home.

*   *   *

---

[6]   Men-nefer . . . Memphis

Chapter 3

Rather than using the main portal, Thut-nefer decides to enter his family home through the side entrance, next to the stables and servants' quarters.

Knocking on the old wooden door, he hears a dog bark, the shuffle of feet, and the painful creaking of the door, as it opens wide.

A young boy steps out from behind the door and immediately recognizes Thut-nefer, quickly hurries over and takes hold of the donkey by the ear.

"Where is your father, young man?" he asks gently. The boy silently points his finger up to the sky, eyes twinkling.

"Up in the palm trees," the boy manages to spit out.

"Good, good," Thut-nefer replies. "Take the donkey to the stable, undo the baskets, and feed him. I'll be right over. When you finish, run down to the corner and fetch me the barber."

Thut-nefer steps inside and is happy to be back home. His eyes follow the boy leading the donkey to the stables, where his mother keeps the three cows and some goats.

Next to the stables, outside the servants' quarters, sit two young girls making thin rope, one end tied to their big toe and the other firmly held in the palm of their hands, twirling the rope as they add bits of coarse palm bark.

This rope, each one cubit in length, had to be strong enough to hold the weight of a bundle of ripe dates. The young girls greet Thut-nefer shyly.

"Your father is up in the trees?" Thut-nefer asks the overseer's daughter.

"Yes, yes, in the lower garden by the lotus pond."

He walks over to the stables and sees his baskets by the door. He retrieves the eel that Nar had given him and rummages for the sling that he had promised the boy.

"I've got you the new sling, but I think I might just keep it," he teasingly calls out to the boy in the stable. Upon hearing this, the youth bursts out in a flash. Thut-nefer tosses him the finely plaited palm bark sling.

"Make sure you keep the birds off our wheat."

The boy unable to hold back his excitement, frantically waves the sling above his head in a mock throw, eyes gleaming like the rays of the sun on a bright morning.

"Go and fetch the barber," Thut-nefer calls to the boy, as he walks towards the kitchen quarters, amidst the happy giggles of the two young girls, now carefully watching the antics of the boy as he runs out the doorway, the family dog close on his heels.

Thut-nefer can't help but smile. He thinks of the Was sceptre that he should be earning soon, not unlike the boy's sling.

The mistress of the house, hearing the commotion in the courtyard, looks out the kitchen window, and sees her son smiling as he approaches.

His unkempt attire horrifies her, though, and she immediately orders someone to fetch water to the main house.

"May a happy day be spent in your honour, Meryt-ra," Thut-nefer greets his mother respectfully, handing her the eel wrapped in an old, dirty linen cloth.

Meryt-ra, mother of two sons, a priest and a scribe, frowns at the eel and then at the young man standing before her.

"What shall I do with you? And with this!" she exclaims with disgust.

Thut-nefer answers back simply, "Cook it for our evening meal, while it's fresh."

Meryt-ra was no simple woman. Being the first wife of the supervisor of scribes at the royal residence, she knew when to be stern and when to be humble.

"These are hard times and every bit helps. Your brother left for his duties at the temple last evening. If he finds out that you brought fish home- . . ."

The young scribe's mother does not finish the sentence, preferring instead to order Thut-nefer to go to the main house and wash up. She also refrains from giving him her usual lecture about fish being unclean.

He quietly strolls through his mother's well-kept garden, taking in several deep breaths of the abundant jasmine so tenderly cultivated there. Thut-nefer stops and closes his eyes for a few moments, remembering the many hours he'd spent there as a child, playing in the family garden.

Sitting down on a nearby stone bench, he ruminates on this place, how he always felt at his best in this garden—secure, happy and at one with nature.

Here, muses Thut-nefer, *the cycle of the world is always constant and in perfect balance; not only because of its great beauty, its protecting shade, its exotic flowers, and its sweet, delicious fruits, but also, because, like the Garden of Reeds[7], it is a natural haven, one which forever blesses all who enter into its midst. Therefore, this garden continually deserves the care and efforts of man.*

---

[7]   paradise

Thut-nefer continues sitting and thinking, grateful for what he and his family had been graced with. Not just the garden, their home, or their place and positions in society, however humble; but for life itself.

Atum, God as the primal Creator, has created Maat, the graceful, elegant order of this universe, reflects Thut-nefer, *and Maat functions always. With absolute accuracy and sublime orchestration, the order and natural balance of things is maintained throughout the universe . . . and I, we, are the better for it.*

The thumping of heavy rope on a palm trunk not far from him stirs Thut-nefer back into reality. He watches as the garden's overseer climbs up into a palm tree, agile as a vervet monkey.

The sun is slowly setting, casting a warm, orange glow on the lotus pond and the palm grove behind it. A gentle breeze, laden with aromatic scents, caresses the garden and all the life in it.

Thut-nefer continues quietly observing. He watches the overseer, who is busy pollinating the young date bundles, his figure seeming like a dancing silhouette high among the branches.

Eventually, Thut-nefer pulls at the rope of the shadouf[8] and lowers the clay jug, which dangles at the end of a strong pole, into the pond. Retrieving the water, he pours it into a small ditch, allowing it to irrigate the neat rows of lettuce and vegetables.

After repeating this several times, he walks down by the papyrus thicket and sits down next to the lotus pond.

Leaning over to touch one of the lotus flowers, all of which are tightly rolled up, Thut-nefer likens them in his mind to the majestic crown of the throne to the Black Earth[9], like the pointed wigs on the tops of many women's heads.

---

[8]   Irrigation device

[9]   Black Earth: Kemet . . . Egypt

In their habitual manner, Thut-nefer thinks to himself, *all of these blossoms are softly waiting for sunrise, and their reunion with their long, lost love.*

A large frog, at the edge of the pond, stares at him, unabashed. Not blinking, Thut-nefer stares back for a moment, eye-to-eye, and then whispers to the frog.

"I know you know, yet you can't or won't divulge anything; because you have a lotus leaf stuffed down your throat. You are the true, the *real* magician of the blue lotus.

Recite by magic and speak with effectiveness, in order to cause the desired result: to reveal your secret to me."

He closes his eyes, falls silent for a moment and reflects. The image of the fat frog lingers in his mind's eye and engulfs his spirit.

The blue lotus is here to protect us from our own foolhardiness and to remind us that the sun rises each day. Each day is a miracle in itself! Yes, man is his own worst enemy, simply by forgetting the simple truths of this world.

Unexpectedly, the frog dives under a large leaf with a quiet splash. Small ripples disturb the balance of the water on the pond's surface.

"That's all it can do, now, is to pull events with it," Thut-nefer whispers hoarsely, his words dispersing with the evening breeze.

"Greetings, o' Sesh," the overseer nods respectfully, the thick palm bark rope neatly coiled up and dangling on his bare shoulder.

He quietly stands waiting for a reply. In his left hand he holds his worn-out sandals, and in his right, a halfa grass bag stuffed with dry pollen stems.

"Greetings, Overseer," Thut-nefer calmly replies. "How are the trees and the land?"

"The palm trees promise a good harvest, as far as I can see. Seven to eight bundles per tree, o' Sesh, and maybe more."

"Your mercy, o' Atum! Make sure you tie the bundle with the pollen stem tightly, in case of a sand storm."

"You know, o' Sesh, what my mother always used to tell us. 'A palm tree full of dates is like a beautiful woman with her magical earrings.'"

Thut-nefer looks up at the overseer and smiles at him. He sees the thin, yet quite muscular man, looking back at him, the colour of his skin resembling the brown bark of the palm.

"Yes, you are right, and you know what my father, your master, used to tell us . . . 'Do not say today is the same as tomorrow, or how will matters come to pass? When tomorrow comes, today is past[10].'"

The overseer looks at Thut-nefer in bewilderment.

"Yes, your father was a very wise man. O' Atum, have mercy on him!"

"Yes, indeed, o' Overseer. Your mother was also very wise. May Atum have mercy on her and us," Thut-nefer answers solemnly, his eyes wandering over to the main house.

"The barber is on his way!" Shendwa's son shouts at the top of his voice, as he races headlong down the garden path.

Thut-nefer stands up, ready to go, and playfully shakes the overseer's shoulder.

"Good work, Shendwa," he slurs appreciatively, knowing only too well the expertise and effort needed to pollinate the young date bundles.

"Come here, boy," Shendwa instructs his son sternly. Pulling him by the arm, he slaps him across the back of his neck. "Don't raise your voice around the master!"

---

[10]   Instruction of Amenemope

Thut-nefer laughs whole-heartedly at the boy's confounded look.

"Let's go to the main house, then, and wait for the barber," Thut-nefer consoles the boy, now smiling from ear to ear.

"I'll go and check on our newborn calf, o' Sesh, and see if its mother is feeding it properly. Did the mistress not tell you?"

"No, not yet, but that's the best thing I've heard all day," Thut-nefer answers happily, grabbing the boy by the neck and gently pushing him in the direction of the main house.

Once at the house Thut-nefer goes straight to the shower room. He disappears behind the reed partition and undoes his kilt carefully. The stone floor feels cool under his feet.

The boy fills a clay jug of warm water, which the girls had brought, and climbs up onto a small platform next to the reed partition. He slowly pours the water over the partition and onto his master's head.

Thut-nefer scrubs his legs and body with a piece of softened palm-bark, while the boy refills the jug.

"More water, boy" he orders, "and when you're finished, fetch me a clean kilt."

Thut-nefer peeks over the reed partition, as he hears the barking of the dog, "Come in, Barber," he calls out cheerfully.

"Greetings, o' Sesh" the barber replies timidly, as he sits down on a reed mat in the outer room and starts unpacking his wooden box.

Each shaving implement, made of the best bronze, shines in the light of the three clay oil lamps. He lovingly polishes the axe-like tool he uses to shave his patrons.

Thut-nefer sits down next to him. The barber inspects the stubble on his chin and head, while he fishes out a small stone flask from his wooden box and pours a little oil onto his hands.

Working in silence, he massages Thut-nefer's head, gently allowing the oil to soak in. With a steady hand, like that of a sculptor putting the finishing touches to a masterpiece, the barber passes his sharp blade over Thut-nefer's head.

He pauses for a moment and wipes the blade gracefully.

"Almost done, o' Sesh," he murmurs involuntarily from the corner of his mouth. "Have some wonderful new jasmine oil, which I'd like you to try."

"Alright, let's try your oil."

The strong scent of jasmine envelopes Thut-nefer and dissipates his drowsiness, as the barber gently applies the oil. He slides his hand over his head and then down onto his chin, feeling the supple and clean shave.

"Good . . . good work," Thut-nefer compliments the man. "Be sure to stop by Shendwa, the overseer, and pick up your payment. Here's a little festival spice for the upcoming feast."

He drops a small amount of spice loosely wrapped in an old coarse linen cloth into the barber's lap. The man's face flashes with delight and gratitude, as he folds the packet carefully, hiding it at the bottom of his box.

Refreshed and revitalized, Thut-nefer briskly leads the way back through the garden towards the kitchen quarters. The cool evening breeze dances over his freshly shaven head, causing him to shiver slightly.

The barber, hugging his wooden box, trots close behind. The delicious aroma of baked bread drifts his way from the smouldering oven, capturing his sense of hunger. Urgently, he decides to take the shortcut to the kitchen.

At the end of the path, Thut-nefer takes a moment to inspect the three conical shaped wheat silos, standing guard like ferocious Nubian soldiers. Built of a mixture of mud and straw, they house the family's indispensable rations.

Two of the three silos stand empty, the small wooden door at the bottom swung open, like a young child's gaping, hungry mouth. Thut-nefer looks away sadly, knowing only too well the consequences of such a state of affairs.

The open air fireplace at the center of the courtyard is ablaze and roaring. In the corner, two ovens, one for baking bread and one for food, are tucked away out of harm's way. Nearby, a stack of palm-tree branches and wood are neatly stacked in small piles.

He takes in the scene. Watching the women do their work so lovingly and diligently makes him feel at ease again, naturally connecting to the earth's dark soil and its wonderful produce.

Thut-nefer sits down cross-legged at the low, three-legged table, joining his mother, who had prepared the evening meal and was waiting for her son to join her. She hands him a thick loaf of fresh bread.

"Eat well, you're looking tired," she coaxes, as she breaks open her own loaf and dips a morsel of bread into the clay pot containing the eel.

"I cooked it in the oven with garlic and lemon, the way you like it."

"It's *so* good, Mother," Thut-nefer manages to utter between mouthfuls. "Yet a touch of festival spices would have livened it up a bit."

"How often do people of the oasis come with their festival spices in these bad times," she laments. "Let alone their wonderful mats, skins and grease of birds!"

"Forgive me, Mother. I didn't mean to upset you. Tomorrow morning, you shall have a full vessel of the finest festival spice in all of Men-nefer."

She looks at her son with a gleam in her eye.

"What? Where will you get me a vessel of festival spice, and of the finest in Men-nefer?"

Thut-nefer simply smiles at her. Curiosity getting the better of her, she asks him in her official "mistress of the house" tone of voice.

"Why do you think you can procure the festival spice? What makes you so sure of yourself?"

"Because I *own* it, and all I have to do is send the boy with the donkey to collect it."

She looks at her son incredulously . . . then in admiration, and finally with suspicion.

"I've been trading," he ventures honestly.

The prolonged silence of his mother, instead of the usual tirade, makes him feel uneasy. Fortunately, she eventually beckons to the overseer's young girl to come and clear the table.

"Take the rest of the eel to your father and bring the fruit basket," she orders, waiting patiently.

Once the girl is gone, Meryt-ra looks at her son solemnly and coughs coldly, her eyes ablaze.

"This harvest you will receive your first duties as scribe, and you must perform them meticulously, just as your father always taught you. It is through this that your dignity and your truth comes alive. O' Atum, light the fires of love in all our hearts."

Thut-nefer can't help but think of Meryt-mi-hapi, her smiling face and the basketful of blue lotus flowers carefully balanced on her head.

"Yes, Mother, I'll do my best to safeguard the honour of our family," he confirms respectfully.

"Come on, then, are you ready to be beaten as usual," she asserts with a smirk on her face, as she pulls the wooden senet board from under the table, ready to give her son a lesson or two in the fine art of the game.

"Think I'll pass tonight, Mother," he replies apologetically. "I'm feeling too tired, and will be off to bed shortly. Have a big day tomorrow."

Thut-nefer gets up painfully, his leg numb from sitting in one place too long. As he moves away from the fire, the darkness of the night engulfs his vision. He pauses for a moment, allowing his eyes to acclimate.

Wishing his mother a goodnight he limps off towards the main house and his room. The reverberation of the croaking frogs and the ear-piercing calls of the crickets accompany him on his walk, and do not cease until he reaches the main door.

Thut-nefer enjoys the cacophony of sound a few moments more, allowing his gaze to sweep across the star-filled sky.

"Di Ankh," he whispers, taking in the majestic sight and simultaneously drawing the hieroglyphic symbol in his mind.

Given life, he muses, *making the written word a living fact.*

Beautiful.

Sighing, Thut-nefer tears himself away from the power of Nut. He steps through the entrance and picks up a lit earthenware oil lamp from the indentation in the wall.

Flickering in the draft, the sputtering oil lamp briefly illuminates the engraving of a lotus blossom hewn in the stone of the doorway. Happy, but tired, he smiles and shuffles lazily to his room.

*　　*　　*

Chapter 4

Thut-nefer, having slipped out early without waiting for his breakfast, walks briskly along the deserted path. He feels the presence of the great and mighty river, long before he can even see it. The smell of the water and the black mud excite his nostrils.

As he nears the banks of the river, a morning haze hangs low in the sky, hugging the river for dear life, seemingly fearful to let go and vanish into oblivion

He can hear the clamorous din of the market in the distance. The noise grows steadily as he approaches.

All the river rats and crocodiles congregate on the banks of the Nile, he ponders, *each one trying to outdo the other with lying speech.*

Thut-nefer chuckles, as he draws near to the first of the vendors, a raggedy old fellow crouching by his vegetables, colourfully displayed in baskets. The young scribe takes a few moments to look over the old man's cabbages, onions, leeks, garlic and radishes.

Upon closer inspection, he notices that most of the man's produce appears rather withered. His toothless grin is contagious, though, and Thut-nefer returns the smile, nods his head "good-bye" and turns back into the throng to try to locate Nar.

He wanders up and down the river's open marketplace, eyeing the diverse wares of countless other river merchants, all shouting to draw his attention.

"Give what you have brought for very sweet sycamore figs!" bellows a vendor next to him. Thut-nefer bends over and inspects the figs in the man's basket.

"I have a little of the finest festival spice," pronounces Thut-nefer, as he lowers his writing utensils to the ground and fishes for the spice in his pouch dangling under his arm.

He hands it and the pouch to the vendor, who in turn, carefully inspects the spices, nods and grunts in satisfaction. The man half-fills the pouch with figs and looks up at Thut-nefer.

"Two more handfuls and choose them from the top of the basket!" Thut-nefer commands.

"O' noble Sesh, these are very, very sweet figs!" The vendor reluctantly adds only one more handful to the pouch and hands it back to his satisfactorily contented customer.

"Very sweet figs, for a very sweet day!" Thut-nefer proclaims jovially, gnawing at one of the figs, as he slips back out into the main flow of the marketplace.

Within a short distance, he sees a small crowd gathering around a man playing a steady rhythm on a small drum. Next to him, a monkey with a rope around its neck dances in circles.

A woman grasps a small child by the hand, stops, and watches the performance. The child is delighted, laughs happily, and jumps up and down, much to the annoyance of the mother.

Is this fig vendor a rat or a crocodile? Thut-nefer wonders. *They're getting harder to distinguish. The rat has begotten a ferocious appetite, just like the crocodile, and the crocodile has become filthy, just like the rat.*

He places two sycamore figs in the earthenware bowl sitting in front of the man playing the drums.

He notices the man's legs, one much shorter than the other. The drumbeat intensifies to a loud crescendo, the monkey ecstatically keeping up to the beat, to the amusement of the onlookers.

Thut-nefer pushes his way out of the crowd, towards the riverbank and quay, in search of his friend.

Suddenly, he spots Nar on the quay, opposite the boat moorings, deep in conversation with some sailors.

"Greetings, o' Sesh!" Nar calls out.

As Thut-nefer approaches the quay from a palm trunk bridge, Nar opens his arms to hug his friend, hoarsely whispering into his ear.

"These sailors are buying up all our spices and are sailing for Khen-khen[11], when the sun is at its highest."

Thut-nefer looks at Nar with amazement, and then whispers back urgently.

"Keep one vessel of the finest for my mother, and when you're finished here, drop it off at home."

"Yes, o' Sesh, it will be done."

Thut-nefer feels the mighty river pulling at the allure of adventure buried within him, as he watches the sailors aboard a ship busily checking their rig. Their sturdy wooden river boats had been loaded with wine jars and other goods.

The supervisor of the ship, with a lotus flower tied around his neck, like a pendant, is standing next to the helm, carefully scrutinizing his men's actions.

---

[11]   upper Egypt

"The sailors are looking for an apprentice who knows the ways of the water," Nar confides. "I would have gone with them, if it wasn't for my sister. Can't leave her alone; she has no one, but me and . . . you."

He stares straight into Thut-nefer's eyes.

"If anything ever happens to me, you will take care of her, won't you?"

"Yes, I will, but only if you tell me the truth. So, if you have decided to go, then it would be better to let me know now. You know, I can read your mind!" Thut-nefer blurts out in jest.

He curiously watches a dead carcass float by. Bloated beyond recognition, Thut-nefer barely makes out its form. Turning his gaze back to Nar he adds, "It's obvious you have an urge to live a life on the river, sailing from one nome to the other, depending on Atum's grace."

"We all depend on Atum's grace," Nar replies respectfully, "and you're not an ordinary scribe, o' Sesh."

Nar picks up a shard from the broken amphorae scattered all over the quay and brusquely throws it at the carcass, hitting it squarely on its swollen belly with a hollow thump.

"You've befriended me and my sister, when I have never seen a scribe make friends with anyone below his caste, let alone eat from the same basket. Your humility is what has earned you my respect!"

"Is it a dead donkey?"

"What?" Nar looks at his friend incredulously.

"The carcass floating in the river."

"Yes, it seems so," Nar squints in the bright sunshine, battling the sun's reflections off the water.

"Rest assured, Nar. Meryt-mi-hapi will be well taken care of. She can stay in my household as long as she pleases. And she can always make herself useful by helping my mother with the chores. You have my word."

"A man is tied down by his tongue and I have no doubt you are a man of your word, o' Sesh," Nar concludes happily, playfully tugging at his friend's arm.

"How can someone be so disparaging and simply throw a dead carcass into the great river?"

"A sign of the times, o' Sesh. Corruption is eating at us, from the inside out."

*   *   *

Thut-nefer suddenly realizes he has spent more time than he's intended to at the river market and quayside, and decides to hurry on to scribe school following a canal that would take him right to the back entrance.

Walking around the building with its majestic papyrus-shaped columns, he enters the building from the front. There, Thut-nefer is heartily greeted by his fellow scribes.

"The master wants to see you!" howls one young scribe.

"And he didn't seem too pleased!" shrieks another.

In defiance, Thut-nefer lifts his wig slightly, just enough to show his freshly shaven head.

An outburst of laughter peals forth from the other scribes' lips, followed by the chanting of his pet name, "Sheshu . . . . Sheshu" . . . followed by even more laughter.

He keeps on walking briskly, through the outer courtyard, through the portal to the inner court, and stops dead in his tracks at the larger than life statue of Thoth, holding the was sceptre[12] and the ankh[13].

Thut-nefer recites a quick prayer and slowly walks to the Masters' hall, filled with dread and anticipation.

---

[12]   Wooden staff. A sign of authority.

[13]   Wooden staff in the shape of the Ankh. A symbol of life.

"As a scribe, you are given the power and knowledge of writing." Thut-nefer hears master scribe Khentika, Supervisor of Scribes in the Men-nefer school, lecturing his pupils.

The young scribe hesitates a moment before entering the large hall and listens to Khentika's monotonous tone.

"First, you must learn the common lettering of the land, so you can perform everyday tasks. Then, if you're graced and talented, you will learn the sacred script. Those who learn it will also have the ability to learn the secrets of the ancient scriptures and the mysteries of the great land of Kemet. Practice your signs well and you will go far."

Thut-nefer enters the hall and stands quietly by a large column, waiting for his master to finish.

"Copy your forefathers, for work is carried out through knowledge. You see, their words endure in writing. Open, that you may read and copy knowledge. Even the expert will become one who is instructed.[14]"

The old scribe sits motionless on his reed mat, wipes his brow, and dismisses his pupils with a flick of his hand.

"Practice your signs!" he shouts at them, as they walk quietly out of the hall.

He beckons Thut-nefer to approach.

"Sit down on my mat, young Sheshu."

"You honour me, my master," Thut-nefer acknowledges in a respectable tone of voice. He sits down cross-legged in front of Khentika and nervously fidgets with his papyrus scrolls.

However, the venerable old man doesn't give Thut-nefer a chance to collect his thoughts and settle down.

"Be skilful in speech, that you may be strong," he advises, looking directly at his disciple.

---

[14]   The Teachings of Merikare

"It is the strength of the tongue, and words are braver than all fighting. None can circumvent a clever man on the mat. A wise man is a school for magnates, and those who are aware of his knowledge do not attack him. Falsehood does not exist near him, but truth comes to him in full essence, after the manner of what the ancestors said.[15]"

Thut-nefer studies the old scribe's face.

Khentika's many wrinkles and the dark patches under his eyes reveal to his student the tired wisdom of a keeper of knowledge.

Yet, his eyes are on fire with these ancient teachings, which beg to find their fulfilment as illumination for the soul, but inevitably only fall on dim hearts and deaf ears.

Thut-nefer tries to concentrate; knowing each word uttered by this man is carefully weighed and delivered in perfect balance of heart and mind, just like the sacred scripture aesthetically placed on a papyrus scroll.

Khentika notices the bewildered look on his apprentice's face.

"Live by the truth and the truth will live by you," he adds light-heartedly, breaking the tension between them.

Thut-nefer inadvertently strokes the Ptah amulet around his neck and manages to smile.

"So, my young Sheshu, are you ready to walk your path?" he asks unperturbed.

"Yes, my master," Thut-nefer answers with a hint of sarcasm "among the crocodiles and rats."

The Old master scribe doesn't bat an eyelid, and keeps staring straight at his pupil.

An image of the frog in the lotus pond flashes through Thut-nefer's mind.

---

[15]   The Teachings of Merikare

"Satire is a good weapon, but dangerous to the user," Khentika counters coolly, "now show me the text I gave you to copy."

Thut-nefer hands him a papyrus scroll and breathes very slowly, in anticipation.

The old scribe examines the scroll carefully and meticulously, taking ample time to scrutinize its contents and quality.

The sudden quiet in the hall is nerve-racking, and Thut-nefer stares at Khentika intensely, waiting for the old scribe to show some sign of approval. His face, though, remains expressionless, as his eyes wander up and down the written script.

The occasional twitch in the old man's left eye causes Thut-nefer to lose faith momentarily.

What was that old herder trying to tell me at the sycamore tree? he reflects. *The fate of a man is placed on his shoulders on the day he is born.*

Yes, another wise man! I wonder how those two would measure up! One has the wisdom and secrets of the sacred scripture, while the other has the rough wisdom of life and the secrets of nature.

Is it possible to combine both into one?

The frog with the leaf stuffed down its throat is unspoken, so that leaves us . . . Thut-nefer imagines the blue lotus flowers blooming in his pond back home.

Khentika finally looks up and clears his throat.

"Yes, I think you're ready. Your sacred script is bold and clear, and I think your heart is in the right place. Read what you wrote."

Thut-nefer takes the scroll from his master and reads aloud:

"I have not encroached upon the fields of others.
I have not added to the weights of the scales.

I have not shifted the pointer of the balance.

I have not carried away the milk from the mouths of children.

I have not driven the cattle away from their pastures.

I have not snared the geese in the goose-pens of the gods.

I have not caught fish with bait made of the bodies of the same kind of fish.

I have not stopped water when it should flow.

I have not made a cutting in a canal of running water.

I have not extinguished a fire when it should burn.

I have not violated the times of offering.

I have not turned back any god at his appearances[16]."

Thut-nefer stops reading and looks up at his master shyly, his stomach feeling like one of those knots he saw the sailors tying on the quayside.

Khentika breaks the silence and utters solemnly, "Yes, it's time you move on. You have now completed your schooling honourably, and you will continue to bring honour to your school, even after you leave.

I will recommend you to the priests at a later time, but for now you will be assigned the duties of a field scribe for the upcoming harvest season.

You shall work for the superintendent of produce. It is he who fixes the grain measure and tax for our lord, King Ibi. Report to the assistant supervisor before you go for all the details."

The old sage falls silent for a moment to catch his breath.

"I present you with a Was sceptre, young Sheshu. Guard it well among your tools, as it represents the truth that comes alive.

---

[16]   From the Book of the Dead

Translated by E.A. Wallis Budge

Brit. Mus. No. 10477, Sheet 22

A young lotus leaf commiserates the original creation of light!

Besides being an important tool out in the field, it will remind you to be your humble self, and of your minute place in the universe, inevitably a key to the cosmos."

He breaks off in mid-sentence and hands Thut-nefer the sceptre, who solemnly accepts it and lays it on his lap.

"There is one more thing I would like you to do, and that is to copy this ancient text, in your best writing, by tomorrow when the sun is at its highest."

The master scribe hands Thut-nefer an unrolled papyrus sheet, who then carefully examines it.

The paper had been tainted by time, yet the symbols felt like they wanted to leap off the page with a life of their own. A shiver runs down his spine.

He looks up at his master curiously, as the hieroglyphics of the sacred text dance around in his mind.

"Yes, fellow scribe, a piece of the ancient script. Honour it with your life."

Thut-nefer carefully binds the papyrus paper and slides it into his utensils box.

Khentika flicks one hand in his usual manner, dismissing him without further thought.

Thut-nefer collects his tools and silently walks out of the large hall.

A sense of relief overcomes him and he feels drained. He reaches into his pouch for a sycamore fig and starts gnawing at it.

"O' Sesh . . . my scribe," a faint voice calls to him.

Thut-nefer swallows the remnant of the fig and looks around. At the far end of the courtyard next to a vast lotus column, in the shade, a young boy sits cross-legged with a wooden writing board on his lap.

The column towers above him, making him even smaller than he actually is. Thut-nefer walks over towards the boy.

"Yes, apprentice? Why are you sitting on your own?"

"The assistant supervisor has beaten me on my hands with his stick, because I didn't write my lessons correctly; and I have to sit here until I finish," the boy states meekly.

"May Atum bless your heart with peace; can you help me with this passage?"

He hands Thut-nefer the offending papyrus sheet, as he kneels down next to the boy. He starts reading slowly and clearly.

"Do not displace the surveyor's marker in the boundaries of the arable land, nor alter the position of the measuring line; do not be greedy for a plot of land, nor overturn the boundaries of a widow.[17]"

Thut-nefer slowly rereads the passage several times, allowing the boy to absorb the material.

He thinks of his own boyhood at the school, all the beatings he had to endure and the humiliations, and all the happy, carefree times. Yes, Khentika is right; it is time to move on.

"Always write the date on top of each sheet," Thut-nefer advises. "Peret[18] III, 2nd year in the reign of King Ibi.

Focus on your writing and don't give up. Remember the ibis . . . Heb! It'll give you the strength to go on."

He fishes two sycamore figs out of his pouch and drops them in the boy's lap. Leaving the boy immersed in his writings, he walks off in search of his friends.

---

[17]   Instructions of Amenemope

[18]   peret: 'The coming forth of the land out of the inundations.'

Chapter 5

Thut-nefer finds his friends sitting in the shade of a Senedjet tree[19] in full blossom, the small, delicate, yellow flowers lighting up the dark green foliage.

He waves the Was sceptre high above his head in triumph and calmly walks up to where they are all sitting. Incredulous, they all stare at him.

"You've got your sceptre already?" Memi asks, admiring his friend's tenacity.

"Yes, my dear friend," Thut-nefer answers, using a purposely pompous tone, trying to hold back his laughter.

Not needing a cue, they all burst out laughing, its echoes tumbling through the empty courtyard with a sense of unabashed ecstasy.

A lease on life had been bestowed, Thut-nefer realizes, with yet another generation of Thoth's scribes huddled together under his shade, like ants waiting under a palm tree for the ripe dates to fall to the ground.

Recognizing this, Thut-nefer ponders aloud, while looking into the eyes of his beloved friends, "What is seen with the naked eye is unreal, while what is not seen is the real."

---

[19]   Acacia Nilotica

Involuntarily looking up into the cloudless blue sky overhead, he wipes the last of his smile off his face.

"So, my friends, shall we proceed and go and see the assistant supervisor for our duties?"

"Lead the way, o' Sesh! May Atum have mercy on us!"

Thut-nefer adjusts his kilt and, holding the Was sceptre in the apt manner, proudly steps forward, a scribe of the holy city of Men-nefer.

"Come on, scribes, lets go and hunt the hippopotamus, perchance we may stumble on our good fortune in these hard times!"

Memi looks nervously at Thut-nefer, his face turning pale with anxiety.

"And remember," asserts Thut-nefer, "that a man's burden is placed on his shoulders before he is born; so, don't fret, as the script has already been written! Let's go and live it . . . our truth that comes alive!"

*   *   *

The four scribes enter the assistant supervisor's chamber silently and in single file.

Ra-hotep is sitting on his reed mat, arranging a pile of unrolled papyrus scrolls with extreme care. He looks at the quartet entering the room from the corner of his eye, taking no notice of them.

They all stand quietly in a neat row, waiting to be addressed.

Ra-hotep's plain features might easily fool most men, but the malevolence glaring from his eyes is unmistakable. Indeed, his malice brands him as a spiteful person among his peers, yet no one can do his job as well as he.

Even his superiors let him be. In return, he often carries much of their work load voluntarily.

Time hangs heavily on the four young scribes' shoulders. Thut-nefer feels Memi's hand begin to twitch, as they stand next to each other. Ra-hotep finally breaks the silence with a dry cough and looks icily at them.

His eyes, sharp and steady as a falcon's, settle on Memi.

A droplet of sweat is slowly meandering down between Ra-hotep's eyebrows and onto his curved nose.

Memi's hand begins to twitch again. The assistant supervisor loves to see his pupils squirm, and the more they show it, the more pressure he applies. Thut-nefer taps his friend's foot with his sandal, hoping to reassure him.

Thut-nefer stares straight back, clenching the Was sceptre tightly and carefully watching the progress of the droplet on Ra-hotep's nose.

"So, you want to call yourselves scribes of the Holy City of Men-nefer! In my opinion, the monkey trainer down in the market has a better chance than you!" he pronounces sarcastically in a loud voice.

"At least he manages to get his monkey to dance to the tune of his drum." He glares at them, steadily working himself up into a frenzy.

"Now listen to me carefully, you scribes!" he shouts, losing his patience.

The droplet of sweat had now reached the tip of his nose and was threatening to fall off the precipice. With a sudden jerk of the back of the hand, Ra-hotep wipes it away.

"This land is in commotion, and no one knows what the result may be. The people's destiny is hidden from speech, sight, and hearing because of dullness, silence being to the fore."

He stands up and stretches his legs. Searching for his sandals, he steps off the reed mat onto the highly polished stone floor. Calmly strolling around the four young scribes, he takes a moment to inspect their general appearance. Disgruntled at their steadfastness, he goes on.

"I show you the land in calamity, for what had never happened has now happened."

Ra-hotep, approaches Thut-nefer and breathes heavily down into his face. The powerful odor of garlic emerging from Ra-hotep's breath causes the young scribe's stomach to turn. However, being resolute as a granite statue weathering a blistering sandstorm, Thut-nefer doesn't bat an eyelid.

"Men will take weapons of war and the land will live in confusion. Men will make arrows of bronze, men will beg for the bread of blood, men will laugh aloud at pain; none will weep at death, none will lie down hungry at death, and a man's heart will think of himself alone."

Ra-hotep unexpectedly retreats back to the security of his reed mat. He sits down directly opposite the four scribes and eyes each one in turn before continuing.

"None will dress hair today; hearts are entirely astray because of it, and a man sits quiet, turning his back, while one man kills another[20]."

He pauses and takes a deep breath. Raising his voice again, Ra-hotep points his finger menacingly at the four scribes.

"Remember this prophecy, as it will help you to adhere to your code as scribes of the holy city of Men-nefer."

Thut-nefer's eyes begin to wander around the assistant supervisor's chamber, as he listens attentively. All the papyri, some rolled up and some folded, are in their proper place, stack upon stack in perfect order. Even his writing board stained in red and black pigment, from hours of work, rests neatly in the corner of the room.

---

[20]   The prophecies of Neferty

"Our land is now two lands and our King has no presence in Khen-khen. In the north east, the land is rich in foreigners and their taxes are being withheld, while the middle island[21] is in chaos. Hard times are upon us . . ."

Ra-hotep hands each scribe a Was sceptre and continues.

"Greatness can be yours by your action, if you have spent your life within the frame of your God[22]."

He pauses for a moment and assigns each scribe his position in a strict official tone.

"Ka-aper and Djet will report to the superintendent of food offerings to help administer the temples and store-rooms with grain. Thut-nefer and Memi will head out to the superintendent of produce to help with the grain measure and tax.

You are now dismissed, o' scribes of the holy city of Men-nefer!"

*　　*　　*

Once outside under the safe canopy of the sendjet tree, the four scribes flop down to the ground with a great sense of relief. Memi starts giggling nervously.

"Is this really it?"

"Greatness can be yours by your action, if you have spent your life within the frame of your God," Ka-aper quietly mimics the icy tone of the superintendent.

Thut-nefer fishes out the last four sycamore figs from his pouch and tosses one to each of his friends. They all look at him with appreciation.

"The truth that comes alive, o' scribes," he ventures, calmly gnawing at his fig. "It seems to me that our great King

---

[21]   centre of Nile delta

[22]   The teachings of a man for his son

Ibi is not achieving Maat. Hapi's flood has been far too low in the past years."

"The king's mediation between the great god and Maat is much too weak. People are hungry and agitated. They have no one to turn too, except themselves, and that opens the door for chaos to enter," intercedes Ka-aper.

"Yes, and this has been causing hunger and unrest as far away as the middle island of the delta where the great river meets the sea," Thut-nefer continues.

Memi interrupts him brusquely, half whispering, half murmuring. "Careful, Sheshu, the trees might have ears!"

"More and more foreigners are settling on our land," he adds as an afterthought, unable to control the boiling rage from within.

Thut-nefer catches the glint in his friend's eyes and falls silent. The four scribes all look at each other in disbelief, while contemplating how they and their immediate families would cope with the famine.

Everybody was affected in some way or other. Only the privileged few close to the King and the governor seemed to be untouched.

Djet interrupts their flow of thoughts by waving his sceptre above his head. Agressively he points it directly at the Sendjeb tree.

"It's the governor and his corrupt force! Greed pure and simple!" he exclaims.

It suddenly dawns on Thut-nefer what Ra-hotep implied when he said that the monkey trainer down at the market was better than them.

He could get his monkey to dance to the tune of his drum. "The governor is playing the drum," he grunts out loud to no one in particular, "and we are dancing to his tune. That's what the assistant supervisor meant."

They all look at Thut-nefer with amazement.

"And that's why we have to live strictly within our code. The benefits of our tradition won't come forth to us, if we don't follow that tradition. I'm beginning to respect that man, Ra-hotep, even though I don't particularly like him much."

Thut-nefer sighs, as he gets up and shoulders his elongated scribe basket. Holding the Was sceptre, he announces to his friends, "I'm heading home with the good tidings of our success. Anyone care to join me for a celebratory meal? The womenfolk are baking fresh bread today!"

"May Atum grant you prosperity and bless your heart," Ka-aper answers for all of them, "And may a happy day be spent in your honour."

*   *   *

Thut-nefer walks solemnly out of the main portal, through the magnificent lotus columns, and takes the path to the nearest ferry that will get him across the canal and homeward bound.

As he approaches the ferry, he sees that the waterlogged reed and papyrus raft has just arrived from a previous crossing and is now docked. Thut-nefer overhears the ferryman having a heated discussion with another man.

"It's the third time you haven't paid your fare. I'm not going to take you across the canal anymore, even if your threats are sharper than the teeth of the crocodile. My hide is thick and the sun has dried it hard. Now, be on your way!"

The ferryman spots Thut-nefer clambering down the slope of the canal and immediately greets him respectfully, lowering his eyes and slightly bowing his head.

"What's the commotion, o' ferryman?"

The boatman looks up, waiting for permission to speak. Thut-nefer looks at him intensely, noticing his left eye is white and glazed over with an eye disease that affects many of his people.

"I have a complaint against this man. He doesn't pay his fare, o' Sesh."

"Do you know him, ferryman?"

"Yes, indeed, noble scribe. He's an artisan's apprentice."

Thut-nefer looks at the apprentice, just as intensely as he did the ferryman, even though the reflection of the sun on the water of the canal temporarily blinds him.

Through the haze of the glare, a little distance further up the canal, he notices a lotus blossom, still partially opened. Thut-nefer feels a strange sense of well-being, as he quietly tries to focus on the flower, hoping to prolong that blissful moment. It eludes him, yet leaves a pleasant tingling sensation at the tip of his fingers.

"Do you see that lotus over there? Both of you look at it for a moment," he orders the two men.

They both look around, the ferryman tilting his head to one side to compensate for his bad eye.

"The lotus brings light," Thut-nefer declares casually, "in these dark times."

The artisan catches Thut-nefer's drift and returns his gaze, crying humbly, "Pronounce your wisdom, o' Sesh, learned man of Thoth!"

"The ferryman shall take you across today. Tomorrow, you shall pay him what you owe him. If you don't, I will consider his complaint valid and send guards with sticks to fetch you. Ferryman, what do you say?"

"I have no further complaint, o' noble Scribe of Thoth."

The ferryman steps onto his raft, lifts the long wooden oar and begins to propel his craft across the canal.

"What do you do, artisan?" Thut-nefer asks, carefully stepping onto the raft, with as much dignity as he can muster.

"We make irtyu,[23] o' Sesh, at the workshop of my master," he answers meekly, also stepping onto the vessel.

The ferryman plunges the oar into the water with great agility, causing only a minimal effect on the surface, each stroke bringing them closer to the other side.

Thut-nefer's gaze wanders over to the spot where he had seen the blue lotus, but suddenly the turquoise sky encroaches on his vision.

Purity of colour is vital, he ponders; *not just in practicing or appreciating art, but if one is to appreciate the world itself. Complete everything in one colour before moving on to the next, a master artisan had once told him, because it is purer. Somehow that always stuck in his mind.*

He smiles and stares straight up above himself at the intensely blue sky.

Irtyu, the color of the heavens, the dominion of the gods, as well as the colour of water in script, the yearly inundation, and the primeval flood . . . all these are represented in one flower's colour. A sacred blue from the brown earth, another miracle.

He braces himself as the raft scrapes it way through some reeds, before sliding smoothly onto the bank.

"We're having trouble acquiring Irytu these days, artisan," he declares, stepping off of the raft. "Why is that?"

"The royal scribes collect everything we produce. The donkey caravans arriving from the deshret[24] have been less

---

[23] Possibly the most famous of all synthetic pigments made in Ancient Egypt. It is still known today as Egyptian Blue.

[24] The red lands i.e. the desert

frequent and smaller," the artisan apprentice answers politely, patiently waiting for his turn to disembark.

"And who is your master?" Thut-nefer inquires, as he begins walking up the path.

The sweet scent of wild spearmint, growing along the canal, accosts his nostrils, causing his nose to twitch.

"Qar, the master Iwen[25] maker," the artisan answers obediently. Thut-nefer nods as he picks up his pace for home.

Not far along the narrow dirt path, Thut-nefer involuntarily stops and steps aside to let a nobleman sitting in a carrying chair pass. The four carriers are drenched in sweat, their flimsy garments plastered to their skin.

The carrying chair is made of the finest cedar wood with gold engravings confirming the high status of its owner. Dressed in handsome linen, the nobleman is bedecked with finery, including a superior quality collar made of turquoise, lapis lazuli and carnelian.

Suddenly, he barks an order to his carriers. "Stop here, you lowly swine herders! I want to speak to this man."

They halt dead in their tracks, not far from where Thut-nefer stands, casually leaning on his Was sceptre.

The nobleman beckons with his hand, which holds a small jar made of alabaster. Four gold rings on his fat fingers shine brightly in the sun.

"You, scribe!' he spits out. "When is the cattle count?"

Thut-nefer looks up at the man perched high in his chair. "In two days time, my lord," he answers politely, hiding his disdain.

The nobleman busily anoints his head with myrrh oil from the small alabaster jar and again barks at his carriers to move on.

---

[25] Colour maker: An artisan whose sole job is to make and mix pigments.

Chapter 6

Thut-nefer enters proudly through the main portal, greeted silently by an old, dark Kushite watchman, standing like a weathered basalt statue he had seen at the main temple entrance.

The thick wooden staff in his right hand betrays the watchman's age; for it is no longer a weapon, but a leaning stick. He stands to attention, as the young scribe walks up the finely polished white stone stairway.

Thut-nefer, ever so familiar with the watchman, looks at the old man tenderly, his wrinkled dark skin still shining. He returns the affectionate gaze and manages to gasp, with a tear in his aging eyes, "You make us proud, young Sesh, and happy!"

Thut-nefer feels like taking the old man in his arms, in appreciation for all the wonderful moments they had spent together since his father had journeyed into the afterlife.

"Two jugs of our best beer for you," he croaks lamely, fighting back the lump in his throat, and quickly disappears into the large hall.

Memories of warm family banquets come to the fore, as Thut-nefer walks up to the large column formed in the shape of a young papyrus shoot. He walks around the column slowly, letting the memories engulf his mind.

Letting out a muffled shout, Thut-nefer waits for the echo of his voice to resound off the polished basalt floor, just as he had often done as a young boy. He stands still, allowing the echo finally to lose itself to the high ceiling.

He can almost hear his father's voice.

"Shut up, boy!" he would often yell, a paternal smile on his face. "Must I bring out the flax whip and give you a good beating?"

Thut-nefer had always sensed his father was joking, assured he would never be hit or abused for such an act. A nostalgic pain engulfs his heart, and he tries to shrug it off as best as he can.

Long gone are the carefree days of my boyhood and the false security attached to it, he reflects.

The large column no longer looks so awesome and foreboding, and the mysteries of life seem more intriguing.

Again, he hears the voice of his father echoing through his mind.

"A man says this speech when he is pure, clean, dressed in fresh clothes, shod in white sandals, painted with eye-paint, anointed with the finest oil of myrrh.[26]"

Thut-nefer thinks of the fat nobleman he had met on his way back, anointing his head with precious myrrh oil . . . only to cover up the musty smell of his carriers shuffling along the dusty path.

Even if he poured the whole jar over his head, it would never hide his impure heart. Impurity has become a disease of the times, devouring men's souls like a worm chewing into the core of a pomegranate, each seed spoiling the one next to it, until the whole fruit splatters to the ground rotten.

---

[26] Chapter 125 of the Book of the Dead
    M. Lichtheim, *Ancient Egyptian Literature*, Vol.2, p.131

Thut-nefer's mood is darkened by such thoughts, and he looks skyward to the sun for illumination and hope through the long and narrow window. A large black crow lands on the windowsill, momentarily casting a shadow upon Thut-nefer's face.

Such mockery is a further sign of the times. Even love has become a struggle, a struggle against oneself.

Turning his head in the direction of the lotus pond, far from sight, but not from his inner vision, he allows the majestic blue lotus in full bloom to accost his mind.

One sweet seed may, indeed, rot and affect others, and yet there is the lotus, bringing out the best in human nature. Whether we know it or not the highest in us cannot but burst out, like a new lotus leaf arising from the thick black mud.

Thut-nefer reluctantly leaves behind all his memories in the hall and shuffles straight to his room, dragging his sandals along the stone floor.

Once inside, Thut-nefer's nostrils immediately pick up the aroma of fresh baked bread wafting through the air, causing his stomach to growl with hunger.

Outside his bedroom window, he hears the water-carriers at work, busy replenishing the pond. Each helps the other unload the heavy water jugs dangling from the wooden pole perched across muscular shoulders.

He can hear Shendwa the overseer barking orders loudly to the men, who take no notice of him, but continue to toil on with their back-breaking labour.

He hears, too, the black waterfowl with their bright red beaks seeking cover in the papyrus thicket, squawking and complaining at the nearby commotion.

Thut-nefer finally turns his attention away from the window and undresses quickly, throwing on his favorite robe and dashing out barefoot in the hope of claiming his fair share of hot, fresh bread.

As he quietly approaches the kitchen courtyard, with its mud brick oven comfortably nestled in the corner, he can hear his mother prodding on the supervisor's wife.

"Now, get on with it, woman, a house with no bread is a sad and mean place. Just like a ship with a broken rudder or a shrine without its god.[27]"

His mother, a benevolent, yet authoritarian figure, stands motionless behind the woman, who sits cross-legged in front of the gaping mouth of the oven.

With one singular motion, she deftly reaches into the oven with a palm branch and fishes out a flat, round loaf, which had temporarily bloated up in the intense heat.

She throws it onto a linen cloth, spread out next to her, with a flick of her wrist, landing it neatly next to the other loaves.

Thut-nefer moves in like a hawk, picks up the steaming loaf, and tosses it up and down in his hands, waiting for the hot air trapped between the two layers to disperse.

He inhales the wonderful aroma, tears the loaf into two and greedily pops a piece into his mouth, singeing his tongue in the process. His mother finally notices his presence, staring at him in amazement.

"What, you're here already?" she gasps.

Thut-nefer swallows the last of the delicious bread, before replying.

"I bring you good tidings, O Meryt-ra! I have honoured you and my father! Today, I received the sceptre and have been assigned my first post as Scribe of the holy city of Men-nefer. Rejoice!"

---

[27]   Hilary Wilson, *Egyptian Food and Drink*, p19

Suddenly, her eyes brighten and fill with sunlight. She turns round and kisses her son on the head, his shoulders and his hands.

Thut-nefer takes a step back to evade her kissing tirade, although his face gleams with pride.

"I will throw a banquet tomorrow in your honour," she exclaims, "with musicians and the finest foods I can muster in these hard times."

"Please, Meryt-ra," Thut-nefer answers solemnly, "we mustn't devastate our storage. People are hungry outside the walls and the harvest is not promising. Thefts are increasing and the harvest isn't even in."

He pauses for a moment to collect his thoughts, and then continues. "While the land is diminishing, its controllers are many. Only the governor and his cronies grow fat off the land."

"Sheshu, stop it!" she cries sternly. "Even if it's only a small banquet, it's part of our family tradition!

Here, take this cup and pour yourself some fresh milk from the milk jar, before we make the cheese. You can find some over there by the stables. It'll calm you down. You probably haven't eaten since this morning!"

Thut-nefer takes the clay mug from his mother's hand and walks over to the stables. He pours himself some milk through the small spout of the round earthen jar, while shaking it gently. Raising the mug to his mouth, he drinks deeply.

"Did the spices arrive which I sent you this morning?" he calls out over the din of the thumping of someone working with a large mortar and pestle in the stables.

He peers through the sombre light, but cannot make out who is busily pounding the bean paste. All he can see is the figure of a woman raising the large wooden pestle above her head and slamming it down into the red granite mortar in a steady and rhythmic motion.

Thump . . . . thump . . . . thump.

Of all the household duties, this was by far the most demanding, taking both skill and stamina.

"Yes, my dear son, I've stored it away!" she echoes back. Go now and see the supervisor's boy. He's had a nasty fall and cut his chin badly."

Thut-nefer stares at his mother, not wanting to acknowledge he'll have to cut short the small, but personal celebration the two were sharing.

"I suppose I must leave, now— . . ." he stammers clumsily.

"Yes, my son. He was asking for you when I left, and refuses to let anyone near him. I myself tried to stop the bleeding, but he won't sit still. His father has sent for the swnw[28], who should be arriving soon. Be so kind and wait for him at the back entrance."

Thut-nefer grabs another loaf straight out of the oven and walks away, tossing it up and down so as not to burn his hands.

At the side portal, he calls for his dog, which appears wagging its tail, happy to see his master. He licks Thut-nefer's hand in excitement.

Thut-nefer gives him a small piece of bread in return, "Where's boy? Where's boy?" he asks the dog. The dog barks, runs towards the servants' living quarters and turns its head looking back to see if his master is following him.

Thut-nefer looks over in the direction and sees the young boy peering out from the doorway of the mud hut. Afraid of being scolded, the boy prefers the shelter of his own home.

The Swnw, who had just arrived, sits down on his haunches and starts to examine the gaping wound in the boy's chin.

---

[28]   doctor

Thut-nefer holds the boy by his shoulders, pinning him down to the reed mat, and attempts to calm him down.

He has lost a significant amount of blood and his face is pale. The swnw retrieves a wooden implement from his box and starts to scrape the wound, very carefully, going deeper with each stroke, until he reaches the bone.

The boy squirms like a catfish in shallow, muddy waters, but Thut-nefer holds on tight.

"The bone is uninjured, no split or perforation to be seen," the Swnw comments, as he looks up at Thut-nefer.

He pauses for a moment to reflect on the best treatment.

"Thou should'st apply to him two strips on the gash. Bind it with fresh meat the first day. Thou should'st treat it afterwards with grease, honey, and lint everyday until he recovers.[29]"

Thut-nefer feels the young boy quiver, as he eases off the pressure of his hold.

He inadvertently thinks of the fat frog sitting in the prow of the bark, sailing through the netherworld, a recurring symbol of resurrection passed down from his childhood schooling.

Thut-nefer fights off a spasm of squeamish shivers crawling up and down his spine at the sight of the boy's open wound. Forcefully, he tightens his grip on the boy again.

The Swnw applies a linen strip on one side of the wound, closing it tightly, and then gently applies the second strip, while holding both ends with his agile fingers.

"Fetch us a piece of fresh meat from the kitchen, Sesh, so I can bind the wound."

"Don't move boy!" Thut-nefer commands, and then shouts an order to one of the girls standing just outside the doorway.

---

[29] Edwin Smith papyrus; Case twenty-seven: Instructions concerning a gaping wound in his chin.

The young girl walks into the room shyly and offers Thut-nefer a small piece of meat in an earthenware bowl. He takes it from her impatiently and hands it to the Swnw, who in turn applies it to the boy's chin.

He then slowly bandages the wound with fresh, clean linen strips, which he fishes out of his wooden medical box.

Finished, the Swnw wipes his brow with an old piece of linen he keeps for that purpose, and then looks into Thut-nefer's eyes.

Thut-nefer can't help but noticing the glint of compassion in the man's gaze, even after years of service to the sick and wounded.

Somehow, Thut-nefer deliberates to himself, *you can never be totally immune to pain, just like the frog in the lotus pond, living in bliss among his beloved lotus, and yet still feels the pain of existence.*

"Will you not stay and share a meal with me, o' Swnw? We have fresh bread still hot from the oven and fried bean paste, which my mother makes superbly."

"It would be my honour, o' Sesh, but I must be going. The butcher near you has hurt his leg, possibly broken it, as he was parading the bull for all to see on the eve of the slaughter. But, I'll be back tomorrow to change the boy's bandages and continue with the treatment."

"Good, good," responds the proud, new initiate. "Then you will honour me by joining my small banquet, o' Swnw, for I have been chosen as a scribe of the holy city of Men-nefer."

"You are a good boy, and you would make your father proud, no doubt. Your father was a good and honourable man, and he helped many people."

The old master smiles down at Thut-nefer and puts his right hand on his shoulder.

"He belonged to a generation who still upheld justice and truth; unlike some of the characters we see roaming our land today, putting nothing but fire in their bellies, defying all the wisdoms of old.

Greed has become a disease, and it is spreading widely from the delta all the way to the source . . . and yet there is no cure to be found. Indeed, we live in hard times!"

Thut-nefer stares back into the face of the obviously troubled sage, identifying his own angst in his elder's frustrated countenance.

"Poor Kemet[30], drying out and on the verge of a famine. Even the King can't uphold his obligations . . . only his empty duties.

Is he judging men? Is he making God content? Is he creating Maat[31] and destroying Isfet[32]?"

The aged healer pauses and looks disheartened back to the young scribe. "But who am I to say? I can only cure certain ailments; just another complainer among the many."

The Wer-Swnw's[33] voice turns into a rasp, and he coughs to clear his throat.

"I must be going, young Sesh. Show me to the portal," he commands, putting his arm around Thut-nefer's shoulder in a gesture of farewell.

*   *   *

Thut-nefer returns from the portal after having escorted the Wer-Swnw, and to his astonishment finds Mery-mi-hapi

---

[30]   Black Earth (Egypt)

[31]   Creating truth and upholding the balance

[32]   Destroying evil

[33]   Master Physician

sitting in front of the stable door, leaning her head against her knees in a sad and forlorn position.

"What are you doing here, girl? Is something the matter?"

"I brought some lotus flowers for your mother, and she asked me to stay and help pound the bean paste. I also came looking for you." Tears begin to stream down her cheeks and she sobs quietly.

Feeling heavy of heart and a lump in his throat, Thut-nefer beckons a premonition buried deep in his gut . . . one he has carried with him, and shared with no one.

There he sees Nar on the wharf talking to the Khen-khen sailors. His dirty linen pouch and his favorite coil of rope dangle from his well built shoulders. A fresh blue lotus is tied around his deeply tanned neck.

The sailors all laugh at him, teasing him about the thinness of his rope. "Nobody makes better rope than me!" Thut-nefer hears Nar shout back cheekily. The sailors, welcoming the unanticipated break in their chores, all join in a chorus of laughter.

I'm going to miss that man, Thut-nefer reflects. I sincerely hope the powerful river doesn't gobble him up. Many a good Northland sailor has vanished sailing up the cataracts.

"Are you not well?" he asks with concern, hoping to draw the girl out of her misery and at the same time, trying to shake off his own sense of foreboding.

Meryt-mi-hapi puts on a brave face, and brushes aside the tears, causing the kohl around her eyes to streak. Thut-nefer looks at her sympathetically, but his fiery eyes prod her on.

"Have you seen Nar?" she feebly asks. "He's nowhere to be found. I thought maybe you would know."

"Yes, I did see him this morning at the market, and then later at the wharf."

He catches his tongue abruptly, thinking that it would be better not to tell her the truth until morning.

"You shall stay with us tonight," he consoles her, "and tomorrow you'll help my mother prepare for our small banquet. Meanwhile, I'll look for your brother; and if anyone can find him, it'll be me."

Mery-mi-hapi smiles meagerly, causing her beautiful black eyes to shine intensely, capturing Thut-nefer's gaze like an all-consuming embrace.

Nothing but the lotus has this kind of effect over me, he admits to himself. *The tingling courses all the way through to my fingers.*

He looks deeply into her eyes, the source of his bliss. *That girl has a special magic about her. It must be from her perpetual contact with the lotus, as if the plant entwines itself around her body and soul, creating a unison of the seen and the unseen, finally blossoming into one singularly beautiful flower.*

Heaving a sigh, entranced by the youthful Mery-mi-hapi, Thut-nefer concludes his reverie.

When I stare into this blue lotus blossom's brilliance, my eyes become imbued with her very essence, her light. When I breathe in her sacred fragrance, my nostrils dilate as if I'm standing at the Other World's garden gate.[34]

"Rise, like Nefertum, from the lotus to the nostrils of Ra![35]" he recites out loud to no one in particular, his eyes still transfixed.

"Have mercy on us, O Atum. We are your feeble creations, groveling in the muddy swamps, looking to you for light. Your

---

[34] Horus, talking about the 'the blue lotus', Graeco-Roman temple of Horus at Djeba, Edfu

[35] From the UNAS pyramid texts

brilliance blinds us; and instead of reaching towards you, we seek relief in our own self-made darkness."

Lifting his head to the sky, he calls out, "May I traverse nature's realm through the gates, carried by Nefertum and the blue lotus scent. For truly, I seek the light."

Meryt-mi-hapi looks at Thut-nefer quizzically, yet with pride, knowing that her brother's friend is now an important person, an official scribe. Her smile broadens.

"Thank you, o' Sesh. May Atum bless your heart and grant you prosperity."

Thut-nefer gently squeezes Meryt-mi-hapi's forearm. In one swift motion, he pulls the young woman to her feet and drags her towards the kitchen.

*   *   *

Chapter 7

Meryt-ra, sets the low, three-legged wooden table in the kitchen courtyard near the oven and beckons to her son to come and sit down.

Once seated, she hands him two warm loaves, which he places on his lap, waiting for her to arrange the rest of the food on the table.

"The hot fried bean paste smells delicious, Mother. It will take some self-control not to descend upon it like a hawk after its prey," he jokes.

Compromising his primal urge to eat, he squeezes some lemon on a few lettuce leaves and begins chewing, patiently waiting for Meryt-ra to bring the rest of the meal.

"Don't wait for me, Sheshu! I'll be eating with the womenfolk later, once we finish baking the bread and making the white cheese." She orders him to commence eating, by waving in the air the small straw mat she uses to strain the cheese.

"I gather you've given your permission to Meryt-mi-hapi to stay with us, until you find her brother," she declares. "You have a kind heart, like your father."

"Yes," he answers between mouthfuls. "I'll tell you about it later. She can help you prepare for tomorrow, as I'll be busy with some work I have to do for my master, Khentika."

Meryt-ra looks at her son adoringly, only now realizing that her boy had become a full-fledged scribe, no longer a child hiding behind her robe, seeking refuge in times of trouble.

"I want you to do something for me, Sheshu," she announces solemnly. "You must go and visit Ptah, He who hears prayers, and offer a gift which I'll prepare for you to take with you in the morning on your way out."

Thut-nefer picks up several small round cakes from the glazed faience bowl and places them in front of him.

Completely lost in thought, he begins nibbling at one absent-mindedly, until he reaches the soft, sweet interior. The sweetness of the sun-dried dates jolts him back to reality.

He looks up at his mother affectionately and realizes that excellence in cooking and baking is in this woman's very breath and *not* localized in her hands.

"Yes, mother, I'll take your offerings to the Mansion of the Soul of Ptah; your wish is my command. But, I must leave early, so have it ready by the time I have my morning meal."

Out of the corner of his eye, Thut-nefer spots Shendwa the overseer hurrying towards him.

He picks up another date cake and begins chewing it, waiting for the overseer to approach. The man stops at the customary distance and waits silently to be summoned.

Thut-nefer beckons to him, while licking his sticky fingers.

"Greetings, o' Sesh," he rasps, short of breath, setting on the ground before him a basketful of lettuce and white radishes.

At Meryt-ra's signal, Meryt-mi-hapi picks up the basket, skillfully balances it on her head, and disappears into the storeroom next to the kitchen.

"Greetings, Shendwa. How's your boy now?"

"He's resting, o' noble Sesh. May Atum give you health."

Thut-nefer looks at Shendwa, bathed in perspiration, making his tanned skin gleam in the orange glow of the approaching sunset.

"Tomorrow, you shall fetch three good musicians for our banquet, and you shall make the necessary preparations."

As Shendwa bows and leaves, Thut-nefer gets up and walks toward the lotus pond, to enjoy the last rays of the sun, before retiring to his room.

Sunset by the pond, just the right time for reflection, he muses.

After sitting quietly for a few minutes with his eyes closed, he soothingly recites. "Awake in peace, You-whose-Face-is-behind; in peace, You-who-looks-behind; in peace, Ferryman of the sky; in peace, Ferryman of Nut; in peace, Ferryman of the gods, in peace[36]."

Thut-nefer continues sitting quietly for a few more minutes, soaking in the serene tranquility of day's end. He slowly opens his now half-closed eyes, then gets up and strolls back down the path to his room.

Upon arriving, he opens the door and stretches, feeling better now that he has meditated, eaten and bathed. His room is well lit by three oil lamps and the cool evening breeze floats through the window, keeping the mosquitoes at bay.

A clay incense burner in the corner drowsily spews out myrrh, a fragrant smoke, delicious to his nostrils and healthily sustaining his emotional balance.

He feels at ease, yet tired. As he lays on his back on the bed, he quietly reflects, *It has been a long stressful day and I'm glad I survived the ordeal at school.*

A vision of the opulent nobleman, who he had encountered on his journey earlier, gnaws at his subconscious, drawing him to face the bottled up emotions it evokes.

---

[36] Pyramid Text of Unas. Utt.270

Among his fellow men, a sleazy desperation prevails, in the search for wealth and power. Shall that be my path forward? Will I too be bogged down in corruption? He contemplates, momentarily doubting himself.

The great unknown swamp sucks at his legs, dragging him deeper and deeper into a quagmire where mercy and love are just meaningless words, like empty clay beer jugs left in the sun to dry.

A voice of wisdom rises in his consciousness, like a lotus rising from the black swamp. *If they would apply the same amount of effort in their search, for the benefit of Kemet and its people, the water would naturally flow again along its predestined course.*

Do not be evil, for patience is good, he's reminded by the voice in his mind. *Make your lasting monument in the love of you.*[37]

Turning his attention outward, Thut-nefer hears the wind whisper through the rustling leaves of the weeping willow standing guard outside his window.

He gently strokes the Ptah amulet dangling around his neck. He whispers to himself, "Ptah has heard my prayer; I must go and give an offering."

Thut-nefer gets up and searches the wooden chest next to his bed for the writing utensils that his father had given him some years back. He pulls out an old-fashioned palette made of a rectangular piece of wood, with two cavities at one end, which hold decrepit, used cakes of black and red ink.

He produces two new dry cakes and fits them into their proper cavities. He reaches into the chest to find a little gum, which he mixes with the pigments, so that they congeal, rather than turn to dust when dry.

---

[37] Teachings of Merikare

In a slot in the middle of the palette, he removes a brush-pen made of rushes, carefully cuts the tip at an angle, and chews it to separate the fibres.

Thut-nefer then moistens the cakes of pigment with the brush, until it acquires the proper texture. Satisfied, he begins to unfold the old papyrus script carefully.

The process of the folding begins at the left-hand edge. He notices that the papyrus is worm-eaten in places, although, fortunately, most of this is blank space.

The fabric is tough and of a good pale colour. The ink is well preserved, and stands out boldly from its background; it varies in colour from the rich black yielded by the freshly charged reed pen to the pale brown of it drying out[38].

The writing, he sees, comes from a good, practiced hand, of the type characteristic of the late Old Kingdom. Thut-nefer scrutinizes the date near the top of the page, and the name and introduction of the writer.

He takes a deep breath and leans over to reach for an oil lamp. *I must have more light*, he thinks to himself, while he nervously gnaws at a large, brown dried doum[39] fruit. *These tasty fruits always help me concentrate whenever I venture into unknown territory.*

He begins to read:

"No one can be saved, until he is born again. If you want to be reborn, purify yourself of the irrational torments of matter.

The first of these is ignorance.

The second is grief.

Third is lack of self-control.

Fourth is desire.

---

[38]   A scribe was able to write about eight or nine signs with one charging of ink.

[39]   doum palms (*Hyphaene thebaica*)

Fifth is injustice.
Sixth is greed.
Seventh is deceit.
Eighth is envy.
Ninth is treachery.
Tenth is anger.
Eleventh is rashness.
Twelfth is malice.

Under these twelve are many more, which force the man who is bound to the prison of the body to suffer from the torments they inflict. But by Atum's mercy, they may all depart and be replaced by understanding.

This is the nature of rebirth. This is the only road to reality. It is the way our ancestors trod to discover Primal Goodness. It is sacred and divine, but a hard path for the soul to travel in a body. For the soul's first step is to struggle against itself, stirring up a civil war.

It is a feud of unity against duality. The one seeks to unite and the other seeks to divide.[40]"

Thut-nefer stops nibbling at the doum fruit for a moment, in order to let what he has just read sink in.

What candor and sincerity, he thinks, marveling at the beauty of its composition. *It points directly to the truth, like the fragrance of a blue lotus awakening all one's senses of reality, dispelling what is unreal.*

Thut-nefer starts to read through the text once more, but stops. Disconcerted, he walks to a nearby window and looks up into the evening sky. A thin crescent moon hangs just over the horizon. He returns to the scripture, and silently recites what he sees before him.

---

[40] The Hermitica

The Cosmos is one, just as the sun is one, the moon is one and the earth is one. Is it right to think there are many Gods? That's absurd! God is one. Atum alone is the creator of all that is immortal and all that is mutable.

If that seems incredible, just consider yourself. You see, speak, hear, touch, taste, walk, think and breathe. It is not a different you who does these various things, but one being who does them all.[41]

Thut-nefer lays back down on his bed, and begins to reflect on the words of wisdom, which have now come lapping up to his shore.

The beautiful lotus flower emerges from the primeval swamp, rising in the darkness, carrying new life and light. The beauty of creation and its irrepressible movement forward, even amongst the present civil strife, leaves no stones unturned.

The hardest stone to be cut with the weakest chisel is the stonecutter's innermost predilection.

Nonetheless, it can be done, so maybe there is hope. O' Atum, have mercy on us. After all, who am I to complain?

*   *   *

---

[41]   Ibid

Chapter 8

Thut-nefer awakens to Meryt-ra gently shaking him by the shoulder. She places a mud tray with his morning meal on the ground next to the bed. A bowl of hot milk with boiled whole wheat, sweetened with honey, is steaming in the cool morning air.

Thut-nefer opens his eyes, slowly focusing himself out of oblivion. The sun has already risen and the first warm rays are stirring life outside.

Somehow, he thinks, *I fell sound asleep in the midst of my reverie. Hm-m . . . I must have needed the rest!*

The songs of many different birds are pleasing to his ear, each trying to out-sing the other, leading to one great hymn of praise.

His mother offers him dried figs, while waiting for the hot milk to cool. He sits up, accepts her gift, and in a hoarse voice manages to croak,

"You spoil me, Mother."

Meryt-ra does not answer, but lets the sparkle in her eyes give her away.

"I have prepared a basket with the offerings, and I suggest you take Meryt-mi-hapi with you to carry them. Send her back immediately, as we have so many things to prepare for the banquet."

"May Ptah, who is south of his wall, refresh your heart through life and very old age," he answers, as he wolfs down his breakfast hungrily, knowing very well that his next meal wouldn't be until much later in the afternoon, when the guests arrive.

He picks up the dried figs and dates from the earthenware bowl and throws them into his linen shoulder pouch.

*   *   *

Within moments of emerging outside, Thut-nefer can feel the presence of Meryt-mi-hapi a few steps behind him, carrying the wicker basket of offerings on her head.

He keeps a fast steady pace and the girl does not fall behind. No words are exchanged, as they continue on their appointed task.

Thut-nefer stops suddenly, turning around to look at her. She stands obediently, silently lowering her gaze to the ground.

"Stay close now, as we're about to plunge into the crowd," he instructs. She looks up at him and their eyes meet. An innocent, foreboding excitement and anticipation exudes from her tanned face.

She steadies the basket on her head with her right arm, while attempting to adjust her long, braided, well-kept hair.

Meryt-mi-hapi's black eyes are on fire, like a carnelian stone reflecting the sun's rays. Thut-nefer feels her excitement rubbing off onto him.

Turning around to the sound of low chanting, they step aside, allowing a column of priests of Ptah, aloof and stern, pass them by, heading for the heart of the largest temple in the city.

Thut-nefer waits a few moments and then starts off again, his heart throbbing quickly to the beat of his footsteps.

He could now see the granite pylons rise from the ground, like colossal papyrus stems of polished stone, standing guard at the entrance of the gigantic temple complex.

Vast hordes of people converge on the public entrance, while hawkers selling last minute offerings try to capture their attention.

Wafts of incense smoke briefly accost his nose, as the gentle breeze plays with the veneered exotic scents, making him feel slightly lightheaded.

His pulse increases again, as he approaches the first giant columns, which seem to simultaneously hold up the sky and the gate.

Men and women crowd tightly together, wild-eyed with exhilaration, as they pass through the entrance.

The coolness of the stone cuts through the morning heat, passing over his face, as if the breath of Ptah himself is rushing by.

As the crowd throngs forward, all moving in one direction, Thut-nefer senses one great heartbeat pulsating inside this colossi temple, the revered mansion of the soul of Ptah. At last, he sees the statue of Ptah, holding the three scepters, the Ankh, the Was and the Djed, while majestically looking down upon Hekuptah[42].

Thut-nefer reverently ponders to himself, as if in meditation upon the image before him, *His omnipresence is universal in all people, all cattle, and all creeping things that live.*

Whatever the eyes see, the ears hear, the nose breathes, goes straight to the heart; the conclusion reached by the heart is then spoken by the tongue.

---

[42]   The temple of Ptah, known as "Mansion of the soul of Ptah"

This is how Ptah commands all into existence and how he became Ta-tenen, 'from whom all life emerges.'

Only Ra and Atum stand above him.

After depositing the basket with the offerings to the concerned priest, Thut-nefer silently says his prayer of thanks and makes his way back to the gate, hoping that Meryt-mi-hapi is still following him.

Feeling too drained to turn around, a blissful peace engulfs his heart, as he heads out of the temple.

Once outside, the blast of light blurs his vision for a moment, making him squint. He spots a shady spot under the neatly lined row of Ished trees[43] a short distance away, and walks slowly across the way.

Deciding to rest for a moment with his back up against a tree, so as to regain his balance and composure, Thut-nefer closes his eyes and feels the silent bliss return to his awareness.

"May your prayers be heard, Master Scribe," a soft-spoken voice calls out to him.

Startled, Thut-nefer realizes that the shady spot already has a dweller, a poor vendor selling Ptah trinkets made of cheap faience.

He looks at the man with interest, sitting on the ground with his back leaning against the tree trunk.

"What are you doing selling your wares so far from the gates?" Thut-nefer asks.

Meryt-mi-hapi approaches silently, sets the empty basket down on the ground, and eyes the vendor's trinkets with wonder. The hawker, sensing her interest, hands her one.

Thut-nefer fishes out a couple of dried dates and a fig from his pouch, placing them in the small, dusty earthenware bowl.

---

[43]   Persea trees, from the avocado family

"Here, take another one, it'll keep the evil eye away and remind you of your visit," the thin man says to Meryt-mi-hapi, "and take care of your master scribe.

He looks to me as a man of honour, unlike the governor's thugs who chase us and then beat us with sticks, unless we pay them bribes to be near the temple.

May Atum blind them! O' Ptah, master of destiny, show them their proper place in the fetid waters of this swamp!"

Spotting three of the governor's thugs approach rapidly from the corner of his eye, the thin man hurriedly stands up and hobbles off, vanishing into the shadow of the trees, leaving no trace of his presence whatsoever.

Thut-nefer watches the lean, strong men with their heavy sticks draw near. Grasping his sceptre tightly, as he did on the day of his final assessment, he stands his ground, not flinching an eyebrow.

Meryt-mi-hapi gasps at the sight of the men, and hastily takes a step back behind Thut-nefer, who boldly stares, straight as the crow flies, into the darkness of the impending foes' eyes[44], agitating his oppressors and causing them to fumble.

"Is the girl with you, Scribe?" the lead man asks harshly, offended by Thut-nefer's cool demeanor.

"Yes, she is part of my household," he answers tranquilly, not allowing his nervousness to float to the surface.

To sustain his equanimity, Thut-nefer holds in his mind a vision of the lotus flower perched on its stem slightly above the surface, not affected by the roughness of the waters below it.

"Where is the hawker who was here?"

---

[44] The Egyptians believe that the heart is the seat of the emotions, the intellect and the character, and thus represents the good or bad aspects of a person's life. Also, they believe the heart is mirrored in one's eyes.

"There is nobody here, but I, resting in the shade of this tree . . . and I must be on my way, as I have much work to do."

Signaling to Meryt-mi-hapi, Thut-nefer steps into the sunshine, leading the way towards the lady of the sycamore, a venerated old tree standing to the south of the Temple of Ptah[45]. The thugs follow him closely, although he ignores them, which only adds fuel to their fire.

Striding as a proud scribe of long standing tradition, Thut-nefer's each step is taken with deliberation and dignity. A small crowd begins to assemble behind him, following in his footsteps, sporadically calling out salutations to him.

The ruffians, disgusted with the spectacle, begin to grumble and wave their sticks menacingly at Thut-nefer and his followers, ordering the crowd to disperse.

Without provocation, all three men start lashing out at the monkey handler with their sticks, violently striking him on his back and his legs. The man collapses to the ground, crying in pain.

The baboon pulls at his chain ferociously, baring his canines, as he senses his master's pain. The throng begins to swell and it engulfs the three men, who by now realize that they are greatly out-numbered.

Not used to seeing such a show of strength and solidarity among the commoners, the governor's men, who are used to ruling by force in these days of turmoil, reluctantly stop beating the monkey handler.

Thut-nefer stops in his tracks and turns around to face the crowd, who are hurling abuses at the governor's men. He raises his voice above the frenzy and begins to recite:

"I have come from my town;

---

[45]   Hathor, titled Lady of the Sycamore, was worshipped throughout ancient Egypt.

I have descended from my nome;
I have done justice for its lord;
I have satisfied him with what he loves.
I spoke truly; I did right;
I spoke fairly; I repeated fairly;
I seized the right moment,
so as to stand well with people.
I judged between two, so as to content them;
I rescued the weak from one stronger than he,
as much as was in my power.
I gave bread to the hungry;
I brought the boatless to land.
I buried him who had no son;
I made a boat for him who lacked one.
I respected my father; I pleased my mother; I raised their children.
So says he whose nickname is Sheshi[46]."

The swarm remains silent and still. All eyes are now glued unto Thut-nefer, as if he had spoken magic words surfacing from a time long lost. Thut-nefer stares back into their bereaved eyes, reflecting to himself with compassion.

The order people have gotten used to has broken down, leaving them groping in the darkness and looking for a beacon of light, no matter how far off. Fear has been instilled into their beings, in place of the rule of law. And, the ancient law proclaims that Maat shall prevail.

A well-kept man draws near to Thut-nefer, somewhat shyly. He introduces himself curtly as Ibeby, a Kherep-ah[47].

---

[46] Miriam Lichtheim, Ancient Egyptian Literature, Volume 1, p. 17.

[47] Priest in the Order of Serqet

"Well said, o' Sesh," he compliments, looking on with admiration. "But take heed, as scribes are killed and their writings are taken away. Woe is me, because of the misery of this time!⁴⁸"

"Fear not, Kherep! Only fear your creator!" Thut-nefer retorts, taking a liking to this man who speaks with such clarity of tongue.

"Your poisons come forth to me. I am Serqet!" declares Ibeby tersely.

Thut-nefer recalls hearing the priests of Serqet occasionally hum these words, before gently tapping a scorpion sting, which causes the venom to rush through the rivers of the body and the victim to lapse into deep breathing.

Shifting his gaze back towards the crowd, he watches silently as they disperse gradually, upon seeing the thugs' retreat, leaving the monkey and its handler lying in the dust.

"Allow me to accompany you along your path, in case the governor's men wait for you," Ibeby offers gently.

"Fine. But before we go," Thut-nefer answers, pleasantly surprised at the man's thoughtfulness, "take a look at that poor man and see that he is well."

The Kherep immediately examines the monkey handler, who sits quietly, rubbing his leg.

Thut-nefer pulls out a dried date and offers it to the baboon, which smoothly grabs it from his hand. Slowly eating it with great relish, the baboon spits out the seed unceremoniously.

"Praise be to Thoth!" Thut-nefer exclaims in wonder as the baboon looks up at him thankfully and sits down quietly next to his master.

"Is the man hurt, Kherep?" Thut-nefer inquires.

---

⁴⁸ Prophecies of Neferti

"His leg is badly bruised and slightly swollen, although nothing seems to be broken. He'll be alright, as long as he rests. Come on; let's move him to the shade of those trees."

"Life, prosperity and health to you both!" the monkey handler calls out hoarsely. "May Atum bless your path and Hathor gladden your heart. Do not worry about me. I am healthy and strong. I will rest for a moment and then be on my way."

The two men move him into the shade and out of harm's way. "I won't forget you, Sesh," he humbly proclaims to Thut-nefer.

Ibeby's round face breaks into a smile, looking over at Thut-nefer. "You seem to have won over some followers today, Scribe."

"And does that include a priest of Serqet?" Thut-nefer replies with a playful smile. "Come on, I'm off to the wharf to look for a friend of mine. Join me if you like; I would enjoy your company."

He turns round searching for Meryt-mi-hapi, only to find her standing behind him, guarding his back like a fierce lioness.

"Praise be to Sekhmet, wife of Ptah!" Thut-nefer exclaims, looking around at his loyal companions in appreciation.

The trio moves on, leaving the man and the baboon resting in the shade, watching them slowly disappear behind the great temple.

"Go straight home, Meryt-mi-hapi" Thut-nefer instructs, as they reach the crossroads, pointing to the path she should take.

She looks at Thut-nefer longingly, her dark eyes proclaiming a silent fellowship etched in their souls.

* * *

Chapter 9

Thut-nefer and Ibeby pick up their pace and head towards the wharf. By the banks of the Nile, the two men pause for a moment, taking in the magic of the great river.

"Let's rest under that weeping willow close to the water," Ibeby suggests.

Thut-nefer nods agreeably, checking for any signs of crocodiles. Finding none, he sits down, taking a deep breath, exhaling the air slowly, releasing with it the accumulated stress of the past several hours.

He looks over at his newfound friend staring vacantly at the flow of the dark waters, his freshly shaven head glittering in the sun's rays.

A certain calm engulfs this man, giving off a sense of balance, as if Maat herself is overseeing the natural order of things. The river flows, the tree grows, the sun shines, and Thut-nefer feels a deep calm tugging at his heart.

Not far from where he is sitting, he spots a group of lotus plants contentedly nestled in a natural cove, protected from the strong river current from the south and the opposing prevalent wind from the north.

Praise is to Maat, thinks Thut-nefer.

An eagle suddenly swoops down majestically, just above the lotus plants, grabbing at some hidden prey with its talons.

Ibeby breaks the silence. "That's the sign, scribe," he pronounces solemnly. "Open your heart and receive Atum's wisdom. Step out from the darkness and let no man or spirit fool you."

Thut-nefer contemplates the Kherep's words before answering, watching the eagle soar back up into the turquoise sky.

"Nefertum . . ." he mumbles, "is the protector of our land, with the power to both destroy and heal. The eagle and the lotus flower perch on your crown. Open the gate and let us through. Remove the veil that's casting a shadow over our eyes, so that dwarves may no longer lead us forlornly like blind men."

Thut-nefer suddenly gets up and tries to reach for a lotus flower, wishing to take a deep breath of its ecstatic aroma. Ibeby places his hand on Thut-nefer's forearm restraining him.

"Did you see what the eagle was after?" he asks.

Thut-nefer looks at him inquisitively, searching his eyes for a clue. The priest stares back, yet reveals nothing, hoping the scribe would catch on to the magic of the moment unfolding before them.

"A frog," he finally concedes with a note of despair. "Hekat[49], you know, Queen of the Heavenly Midwives, wears a sacred amulet in the shape of a frog that bears the inscription, 'I am the Resurrection!'"

Dumbfounded, Thut-nefer looks at the shallow waters and puddles along the bank, teeming with thousands of tadpoles and young frogs.

"Fruitfulness and the coming of life," he reflects aloud. "So the frog represents resurrection, just like the lotus bringing light up from the darkness of the swamp."

---

[49]   Hekat: the frog headed goddess of child birth

Pausing, Thut-nefer thinks of the fat frog in his pond back home, taunting him with its deep croaks.

Ibeby breaks the silence.

"You are looking for a friend along the river?"

"Yes, indeed, a young fisherman by the name of Nar."

"Who has vanished recently?"

"Yes, he is the brother of the young girl who was with me at the temple."

"And you would like to know where he is?"

Ibeby looks at Thut-nefer squarely in the face, his pointed nose twitching.

"Well, then, see if you can collect a little wood and a few palm branches to light a fire."

Ibeby fiddles in his pouch and produces his fire stock and drill, then begins to expertly twirl the drill. Thut-nefer, meanwhile, gets up and looks around for some dry scrub.

In a few moments, he returns with an armful and stacks it, carefully facilitating the task for the priest.

The dry underbrush does not take long to light, and soon the flames are roaring.

"Now, sit down, keep quiet and keep your eyes on the river," Ibeby orders Thut-nefer, while he rummages through his pouch again, retrieving what looks like the dried head of a frog.

"Prescription to make them speak: you put a frog's head on the brazier, and then they speak.[50]"

With a quick, whipping motion, Ibeby dramatically throws the head onto the embers.

"Where is Nar, son of the fishermen?" Ibeby asks aloud, and then falls silent.

Thut-nefer stares deeply into the river, watching the ripples of the current playing along the muddy banks.

---

[50]   From the Demotic magical papyrus. London

Everything seems to be at a standstill in his mind, except the mighty river before him, flowing endlessly from time immemorial, bringing with it its life force.

"*I am the resurrection!*" it screams at him, making him feel like one of those ripples helplessly washed ashore, one moment here and then the next gone.

Nar's smiling face appears in his mind, and beyond reason, Thut-nefer feels his presence, the warmth of his heart reaching out to him.

Several small fishing boats appear to him, too, tied up together along the riverbank under an old weeping willow. And stronger than before, Nar's smiling face.

"The crocodiles are coming!" Ibeby hisses urgently. "It's time to move on. The charm, which you pronounce when you dismiss them to their place, is this: good dispatch, joyful dispatch![51] Come on, o' Sesh, let's move."

Ibeby puts out the fire quickly, throws his pouch over his head, and they both move to higher ground. Thut-nefer looks over his shoulder at the crocodiles stealthily approaching.

"Praise to Atum, creator of all living things!" he yells at the top of his voice.

*   *   *

Thut-nefer and Ibeby follow the small path towards the quay, walking in silence, each one caught up in his own thoughts.

A little further downstream, Thut-nefer notices an old weeping willow, its branches drooping down into the river, as if begging for forgiveness from the torrent dragging at its limbs.

---

[51]   From the Demotic magical papyrus. London

He had walked this path many times before, but had never noted this impressive tree.

Under the willow's branches, well camouflaged, Thut-nefer could barely make out several fishing boats made of reed and papyrus, all lashed up together to form a small platform on the water, big enough to hold a small group of fishermen.

He could see their heads bobbing up and down, as each gust of wind brought in a small wave. Two of the men stand on the platform bent over, busily repairing their nets and traps, while a third is lying on his back, drinking beer from an earthenware jug.

Ibeby stops and puts his arm on Thut-nefer's shoulder.

"Look, the boats and the tree. The spirits have spoken. These men will know the whereabouts of your friend. Come on, let's go and speak to them," he whispers excitedly, as he leaves the path towards the bank.

Walking around several thickets of papyrus, Thut-nefer closes in on his friend's heels.

"Greetings, o' fishermen! I am Ibeby, priest of Serqet, and I wish to speak to your elder."

"Greetings, master Kherep," one of the men repairing the nets answers solemnly.

"Our father is ill," he continues, a sadness palpable in his voice. "A hippo overturned one of our boats last night, and he was bitten while he was in the water.

We've been praying for help, as our father is a good man who never hurts anyone. Please, help him. May Atum grant you life, prosperity and health! We are only poor fishermen, but we can pay for your services with some of our catch."

Ibeby looks over at Thut-nefer and beckons. "Come, help me with this injured man."

They both clamber onboard, careful not to upset the equilibrium of the scanty floats.

The musty smell of the river and the fish being cleaned and salted overpower Thut-nefer's sense of smell. He looks at the wounded fisherman and tries to appease him with some kind words.

The man's eyes respond to the kindness with a gleam of hope. His rough hand, covered in fish scales, grabs hold of Thut-nefer's arm and squeezes gently.

Ibeby busily cleans the wound and applies sycamore seeds mixed with sweet beer. He wraps the wound with clean linen strips and murmurs under his breath,

"Magic is effective together with medicine. Medicine is effective together with magic.[52]"

Only Thut-nefer understands the Kherep's incomprehensive mutterings and looks at the priest bemused, knowing only too well that this fisherman needs to be treated by a swnw.

But in these times, he quietly thinks to himself, *the lines of definition are very hazy, indeed.*

The head fisherman looks at the pair thankfully, raises his arms above his head, and exclaims hoarsely.

"Praise be to Atum! What can we do to repay your kindness?"

"We're looking for my friend, Nar, a man of your people. He's been missing since yesterday. Do you know of him?"

"Nar and his sister Meryt-mi-hapi. Yes, he's sailed with the Khen-khen trade ship south to the nome of the Two Sceptres.[53] We warned him against going south in these unstable times, but he didn't listen.

His reply, in a raving, feverish manner, as if a crocodile was about to overturn his small boat, was something like this."

---

[52] From the Ebers papyrus
[53] Oxyrunchus

The man breaks into a sweat and lapses into his fishermen's dialect.

"We must practice much before we manage to deal with the frog and its resurrection, yes; especially making sure your craft is well battened down, your nerves steady, no ripples on the surface of the pond, no empty beer jugs on the trail."

The fisherman pauses briefly. Raising his arm high above his head, he dramatically waits for the right moment to carry on.

"Steady, mate! Bark out your order!"

He strikes the side of the papyrus boat and leaves his arm dangling in the water.

"After all, we're all sailing towards the source . . . o' creator of the heavens, bless our path . . . we are only meek, humble beings stumbling and groping in the darkness."

The wounded man stops and takes a deep breath. In agony, he reaches out for the earthenware jug and guzzles down what's left of the beer.

Wiping off the froth from his mouth with the back of his hand, he stares directly at the scribe.

Thut-nefer sits mute, stunned by his words. With a deep look of amazement, he mulls over what he has just heard.

Didn't think Nar had it in him. Sounds more like jumbled up feverish dreams!

"Thank you, fisherman," Ibeby answers, as he pulls Thut-nefer back onto the riverbank.

Thut-nefer quietly utters to Ibeby, "I feel as if my feet are not touching the earth, as though I'm floating in the air just above the surface of the water, watching my brown-gray mirror image dancing softly in the current."

Ibeby shakes him. "Break out of it, scribe! Do not let the spirits get a hold of you! Dispatch him!"

Thut-nefer hears the hoarse whisper, as if it were coming from a place where time is at a standstill.

What are the words? he tries to recall, his mind shadowy, yet somehow so clear. *I feel like I'm watching myself from a distance.*

"Good dispatch, joyful dispatch!" he manages to blurt out loudly, as he leans heavily onto the priest of Serqet to regain his sense of groundedness.

"Are you well, o' Sesh?"

"Yes, good, good!" Thut-nefer answers, slightly dazed.

"You had a good lesson today, scribe! Always follow your heart, my friend, for the heart gives man's life its direction. The west seeks to hide from him who follows his heart. The heart is a god; the stomach is its shrine.[54]"

Thut-nefer, now steady on his feet again, bids his newfound companion goodbye at the dusty intersection just before the wharf, and begins to walk towards scribe school.

He hesitates for a moment and turns around to face the priest, who stands peacefully watching him amble away.

"Would you honour me and join my small banquet, o' priest of Serqet?"

"It would be my honor, o' Scribe of the Holy city of Men-nefer!"

A smile creeps onto his face, and his nose begins to twitch. The priest brandishes his heavy wooden staff in farewell and saunters off, his thin frame appearing even thinner in his long, sleeveless, coarse linen robe.

Thut-nefer could hear the jingling of all the amulets dangling from Ibeby's neck and staff, even from where he stood.

His worn-out sandals kick up a small cloud of dust, as he shuffles along quickly towards the market by the quay, undoubtedly looking for people who would need his services.

---

[54] The inscription of Nebneteru

M. Lichtheim, *Ancient Egyptian Literature*, Volume III, p. 22

"Meet me at the ferry at mid-afternoon," Thut-nefer shouts at the retreating figure, as he raises his sceptre in return.

*   *   *

"Where have you been? You're very late," Memi asks. "The other scribes couldn't wait for you any longer and had to leave."

"I had to pass by the temple of Ptah and drop off some offerings for my mother," Thut-nefer replies, with a grin on his face. "Sorry to keep you waiting."

He settles down onto his haunches in the shade of the sendjet tree and looks into his friend's eyes.

"We just heard there was some kind of commotion at the temple," Memi asks. "What happened?"

He watches as his friend fiddles with his writing equipment. Once satisfied everything was in its right place he answers.

"I'll tell you about it later, if you don't mind. I'm looking for a papyrus that Khentiki gave me to copy. I hope I haven't left it at home."

Memi grabs hold of Thut-nefer's arm and squeezes it gently in an effort to capture his attention.

"Khentiki has been taken ill," he remarks sadly. "We saw him earlier, as they accompanied him from school, presumably to his home. It's quiet and nobody wants to talk about it."

Memi stands uncomfortably before Thut-nefer for a few silent moments.

"To make matters worse, the superintendent is in a foul mood and very distraught. All he did was shout at us! Lucky for you, he didn't seem to have missed your absence."

He stares down at Thut-nefer, who sits before him, quietly reflecting.

"You and I have the cattle count at Userkaf's sun temple. I think he was trying to get rid of us quickly and as far away as possible."

Thut-nefer looks at Memi baffled.

"But, he was fine, yesterday. Did you see who was accompanying him? Were they scribes or others?"

"As far as I could tell, it was two scribes from school and two burly men not known to us," Memi replies, sliding a finger under his wig to scratch his head.

"Come, Sesh, walk with me to the ferry and I'll tell you about the commotion at the Ptah temple and my encounter with a priest of Serqet."

Getting up from his haunches, Thut-nefer asks, "Can you remember what our master scribe used to tell us after each lesson? The soul goes to the place it knows and does not stray on yesterday's road."

Thut-nefer falls silent for a moment, trying to recall the exact words. Memi picks up the queue and continues in his soft-spoken voice.

"Beautify your mansion in the West, embellish your place in the necropolis with straightforwardness and just dealing, for it is on that which their hearts rely; more acceptable is the character of the straightforward man than the ox of the wrongdoer.[55]"

"Yes, Memi, well spoken! May Ptah who is south of his wall refresh your heart through life and very old age. Our dear master! May Atum grant him peace and health!"

"Look! The one who dances is crawling up on your wig!" Memi laughs and points at the green praying mantis raising itself on its hind legs on top of Thut-nefer's wig.

---

[55] Teachings of Merikare

He reaches over slowly and picks up the mantis in the palm of his hand, looking at it with great fascination, gradually moving his hand towards the nearest leaf of the tree. There, he gently disposes of it.

"You see, you must be blessed, o noble Sesh," he chortles, teasing his friend. "Come, let us be merry, for the one who dances has spoken!"

Memi takes Thut-nefer by the arm and they both set off, side by side, on the narrow path that leads to the ferry. They both laugh heartily, occasionally dodging the branches of the castor oil trees gracefully lining the course.

"Rise like Nefertum from the blue lotus to the nostrils of Ra!" Thut-nefer exclaims forcefully, leading the way down the embankment to the waiting ferryman.

"Greetings, ferryman!" he calls out jovially, inadvertently scaring off a pair of kingfishers perched on a nearby branch overlooking the canal.

The flutter of their wings cause a ripple effect on the surface, as they swoop low over the brownish grey water of the canal, in search of a quieter location.

"Greetings, o' noble Sesh!" the ferryman answers loudly, as he propels his boat from across the canal, singing:

"My boat sails downstream
In time to the stroke of the oarsmen.

A bunch of reeds is on my shoulder,
And I am travelling to Memphis, 'Life of the Two Lands.'

And I shall say to the god Ptah, Lord of Truth:
"Give me my fair one tonight."

The god Ptah is her tuft of reeds,
The goddess Sekhmet is her posy of blossoms,

The goddess Earit is her budding lotus,
The god Nefertum is her blooming flower,

My love will be happy!

The dawn irradiates her beauty.
Memphis is a crop of pomegranates,

Placed before the god with the handsome countenance.[56]"

*　　*　　*

---

[56]   Chester Beatty Papyrus

Chapter 10

As Thut-nefer enters the great hall in order to check on the last finishing touches for the upcoming festivity, he is flabbergasted with delight.

The family's banquet hall looks to him like a spruced up bride, the basalt floor shining like the kohl adorning her wide and beautiful eyes.

One large column seems to show off its strength by independently holding up the high roof, allowing the many windows to let in the glorious sunrays uninterrupted, dashing against the painted upper walls.

It has been years since he's seen this hall come alive again, and it feels good. *Nothing like a small banquet to raise one's spirits,* he thinks to himself, smiling.

Meryt-ra, already dressed in her finest clothing, rushes back and forth across the hall, putting in the finishing touches on the five tables she had exquisitely laid out, each seating reflecting extremely tasteful precision.

Only a person of her stature could know how everything fits together, so as to achieve the perfect balance in banquet etiquette.

Every flower had its proper place, every blue faience bowl of fruit, every drinking vessel; nothing has been left to coincidence.

Behind her, Meryt-mi-hapi is busily arranging the flower collars of blue and white lotus, each carefully entwined in a mesh of palm leaves, ready to offer to the guests as they arrive.

Her simple, lined, linen dress sticks to her body, allowing her beautiful curvature to come to the fore.

The necklace of blue faience around her neck, the two ptah amulets around her wrists and a lotus blossom carefully tied in her hair inspire in Thut-nefer a surge of longing, as he eyes her from across the hall.

Casually strolling over to the corner of the banquet hall harboring the musicians, he pleasantly greets them.

The elderly flautist solemnly returns the greetings, introducing the other musicians, the drummers, the harpist and, finally, the three young girls who will be clapping and dancing.

The flautist begins to play a soft tune on his reed pipe, puffing out his cheeks with air. The drummers waiting attentively for their queue rub the skin on their drums to keep them tuned.

Meryt-ra beckons to her son from across the hall, wishing to give him last-minute instructions and the seating arrangements of their guests.

"You look beautiful, Mother," he whispers, as he kisses her on both shoulders.

She beams with pride and adjusts her large necklace of carnelian, lapis lazuli and turquoise stones tucked in neat rows. Around each upper arm, she wears two golden cobras swallowing their tails.

"Your uncle Perneb and, of course, our neighbours are coming, too; so please, seat them at that table," she confides surreptitiously to her son, steering his attention with a nod in the table's direction.

"That is, once you have greeted them. Try to be friendly to Keki and his daughter. She is coming specially to see you."

Thut-nefer spies a sneaky gleam in her eyes, as she adds, "Isn't it time that you open your own house?"

Thut-nefer prefers not to answer, staying silent. From the corner of his eye, he spots Memi and Ibeby at the entrance, waiting to be ushered in.

Memi had gone home to change and collect the priest of Serqet from the ferry. The Kherep looked as wild as ever when he arrived, like a scorpion that had just left his shelter in search of any passing prey.

His nose constantly twitching, his dark eyes on fire, the priest strides in, a formidable figure with all his amulets dangling. In contrast, Memi, deriving from a long line of scribes, stands with his usual soft arrogance.

Memi politely greets the mistress of the house with his customary well-bred courtesy. Almost immediately, he engages Meryt-ra in a tirade of flattery, causing her to blush.

Thut-nefer grabs two flower collars from Meryt-mi-hapi, and unintentionally brushes against her, unleashing a silent, yet pronounced sense of arousal in both their bodies.

His fingers begin tingling at their tips, but he tries to ignore the sensation. However, the fragrance of the lotus flower garland only confuses him even more.

Love is light and light is love, he quickly ponders.

Suddenly coming to everybody's rescue, a musician opens his voice to the hall and begins to sing in a lamenting tone.

"The voice of the dove is calling,
It says: 'It's day! Where are you?

O bird, stop scolding me!
I found my brother on his bed,
My heart was overjoyed.'

Each said: 'I shall not leave you,
My hand is in your hand;

You and I shall wander
In all the places fair.[57]'"

As he croons out each phrase, his melody is steadied by a soft chorus of female singers.

Thut-nefer slowly places a garland around his friends' necks and greets them good-humoredly, leading them to a table closest to the musicians. One-by-one, his guests arrive, his uncle Perneb followed by Keki and his daughter, each receiving the same warm welcome.

Finally settling down at his table, Thut-nefer picks up a whole duck and breaks it into four portions with his hands, placing it in on a blue faience plate with a fancy lotus design, nodding to his friends to help themselves.

Memi reaches over and hands him a loaf of bread, quietly observing the glowing smile on his face. The priest timidly passes around the lettuce and cucumbers, and they all heartily dig into the delicious meal.

Meryt-mi-hapi wanders over to their table with a bowl of stuffed pigeons that his mother had sent over. She waits silently for instructions.

Thut-nefer looks up at her, only now noticing her coarse, yet stunning beauty. Her dark brown skin, deeply tanned by the eternal sun, enhances the white linen of her dress.

He takes the bowl of pigeons, stuffed with spices and boiled bulgur, and places them on the plate with the duck.

---

[57] Love poem from Papyrus Harris 500. M. Lichtheim, *Ancient Egyptian Literature*, Vol. 2, pp. 190f

Without speaking a word she takes the empty bowl and disappears softly like a cat stalking in the underbrush, only the soft rattle of her necklace betraying her presence.

The musicians are now softly following the lead of the harpist, waiting for the guests to finish their meal before they pick up the tempo.

Thut-nefer looks over at the other guests sampling the various dishes with gusto. His uncle Perneb is in a deep conversation with their neighbour, both of them occasionally breaking into raucous laughter.

The neighbour's daughter daintily plucks the succulent flesh from a roasted pigeon; she looks somewhat bored, her eyes wandering over to Thut-nefer's table.

Their eyes meet for a moment, before she looks down at her plate. Thut-nefer can see that she is well-bred, her skin pale from being indoors most of the time.

Her dress is made of the finest linen, sticking to her small, but slightly plump body. The jewelry that adorns her is of the finest quality and she wears it with the style of the times.

The large necklace around her neck, of white and blue beads set in neat rows, is bound together by highly polished carnelian stones. The lavish beads serve only to enhance her pale complexion.

Her long hair is plaited in strands, decoratively interwoven with turquoise faience beads and tightly held together by a linen headband, which itself is adorned with small lotus amulets.

A scribe at the royal house, her father, finds it important to keep up her image as that would naturally reflect back onto him.

Yet, her eyes, Thut-nefer notices, made up beautifully with green kohl, seem to lack the fiery appetite for the lust of life, in contrast to the bright yellow stamens of the lotus garland dangling around her neck.

The soft music and the familial atmosphere evoke memories for Thut-nefer . . . of his father. When he'd died, Neferefre had begun on his journey into the underworld with a pure heart, according to Thut-nefer's entire family. He pauses to recall some ancient teachings.

The heart is a record of a person's moral past weighed by Anubis against a feather representing Maat. If found too heavy it was devoured by the monster Ammit, terminating its owner for eternity.

The heart of Osiris hath in very truth been weighed, and his Heart-soul hath borne testimony on his behalf; his heart hath been found right by the trial in the Great Balance.

There hath not been found any wickedness in him; he hath not wasted the offerings which have been made in the temples;

He hath not committed any evil act; and he hath not set his mouth in motion with words of evil whilst he was upon earth.[58]

Yet, now his father was gone.

A sense of false security had settled in the house, like a young mouse in the open fields, unaware of the hovering hawk high in the sky, waiting for the opportune moment to swoop down for the kill.

His uncle Perneb, Meryt-ra's half brother, is a handsome man and his self-confidence portrays his high position. As Sab-ad-mer, the inspector of the canals, he is a commander of men, ruthless when barking out his orders and never takes no as an answer.

He had tried to replace his father, but his authoritarian manner had soon caused deep resentment within the immediate family, resulting in his brother joining the priests of Ptah.

---

[58]   The speech of Thoth. Budge *The Papyrus of Ani*

As a childless man, Perneb, attempts to rule the family as ruthlessly as he would one of his gang of labourers, who tirelessly toil to dig out clogged irrigation canals.

His mother has absolutely no say whatsoever whenever he is around, merely chanting in, "Your uncle knows best." And this makes her look meek and downtrodden in the eyes of her household. This upset Thut-nefer, pushing him to rebel against his uncle's firm hand.

Thut-nefer had always tried to evade Perneb, as much as possible, escaping into the open spaces and living his life with the simple people, feeling more at ease that way.

This would only infuriate his uncle even more, causing him to rage like a hawk among the sparrows and doves, creating a deep chasm amongst the family.

"You're from a noble lineage," he would always bellow in his huffed up voice, eyeing Thut-nefer with a cold, demeaning look. "Why are you living amongst the scavengers? Are we depriving you of your morsel of bread?"

Thut-nefer can't help but think of the fat nobleman perched high in his carrying chair, pouring the precious oil of myrrh on his head, only to avoid the natural smells of nature arising from below.

Where are the old traditions of the kings of old walking barefoot, followed faithfully by their young sandal-bearers! Thut-nefer wonders.

Perneb notices Thut-nefer's's furtive glances, and orders, rather than beckons, the young scribe to come and join him at his table.

Ibeby looks up at Thut-nefer cautiously, sensing the malaise in the air. His nose begins to twitch and his eyes warn Thut-nefer of impeding disaster.

"Remember this afternoon at the river," he whispers. "Float yourself above him and his poison won't affect you."

He hands him an amulet inconspicuously from under the table, just as Thut-nefer gets up.

"Bring two jugs of beer, Meryt-mi-hapi, for my friends," Thut-nefer orders loudly, raising his voice above the sound of the music.

"So . . . young scribe of the holy city of Men-nefer," Perneb asks sarcastically with a scowl on his face. "Are we now congregating with rogue priests of Serqet?"

Thut-nefer stays calm, his fist clenched tightly around the amulet, not wanting to be drawn into a spat he has no chance of winning.

"No, my uncle," he says passively, hoping to ride out the upcoming wave.

Thut-nefer politely greets Keki, the neighbour, and his daughter, noticing the young girl's eyes looking him up and down with keen interest. The instant their eyes meet, she looks away, pretending not to be bothered.

"Greetings, Sheshu! You've honored your father with your success," the scribe of the royal residence casually answers.

Keki is a rather plump man, apparently too fond of life's sweet delicacies. He is sweating heavily at the brow, a sure sign of his indulgence in his mother's excellent cuisine.

His beady eyes shift to and fro from Thut-nefer to the over laden plate placed before him. The scribe of the royal residence stuffs half a roasted pigeon into his mouth with no further ado.

Meryt-ra gently beckons to her son to sit down, and then offers him a plate of delicacies she had prepared for the distinguished guests. Thut-nefer declines, but accepts a chalice made of intricate design, which contains a delicious wine his mother had carefully hoarded.

He sips at the wine slowly, enjoying its robust sweetness and the tingling sensation at the back of his throat.

Perneb breaks the silence in his usual stiff manner, addressing his nephew head on. For him, there was never a spare moment for a friendly chat, especially with whoever he considered to be beneath him.

"The Scribe of the Royal Residence has invited us to a day of fowling soon. It is my honor to graciously accept on both of our behalves."

He pauses for a moment and takes a large mouthful of wine from his faience chalice, and swirls it in his mouth before swallowing.

Thut-nefer makes use of the moment and unclenches his fist to look at the amulet the priest had just given him. It is a small green frog.

Ibeby's face flashes before him, smiling, his two front teeth black with decay. *The resurrection, remember the resurrection, he seems to be saying*, muses Thut-nefer.

He clenches his fist, once again, around this small, yet precious gift . . . and with it, his vision.

"We will be building a marsh boat for the occasion and, as a gift to his honour, you will be supervising its construction."

"But, my uncle, I've been assigned my duties- . . ." Thut-nefer tries to interrupt, but to no avail. Perneb immediately turns his attention elsewhere, as if Thut-nefer wasn't even sitting at the table.

"Besides it's a good opportunity for you to meet the governor and his magistrates," he adds as a closing remark; again, without even glancing in his nephew's direction.

The crocodiles and the rats are infesting our noble river, thinks Thut-nefer. *No wonder the great river flooding is so low. O' Atum, have mercy on us!*

Keki interrupts Thut-nefer's thoughts, "We're laying the foundation markers for King Ibi's pyramid, and the deposits are to be laid soon in their secret resting places.

All the materials have been marked with the King's name, according to the traditions of old. I'm going to put your name down for the head of a work gang."

Thut-nefer shrugs quietly, and nods assent to the duties being placed upon him.

"I know you'll be very busy with the harvest," continues Keki, "but once you finish, I expect you to report to me at the Royal Residence for your instructions.

We need young dynamic scribes like you, Sheshu, as the older ones have gotten fat and lazy!" He laughs deeply, making the three-legged table rattle.

Unaware of his own stoutness, he quickly shoves the rest of the pigeon in his mouth, crunching the bones with his teeth, like a granite mortar and pestle.

"You honour us, o' noble Sesh," Perneb answers immediately, delivered with deliberate pomp and flattery, as is customary in the Royal Residence.

Thut-nefer's eyes wander over to Keki's daughter. A wry smile creeps onto her face, although she attempts to disguise it as a look of concern. It suddenly dawns on him this could all be of her doing, manipulating her father to determine his fate, entwining his with hers!

That old herdsman at the sycamore is no one's fool, Thut-nefer realizes. *The fate of a man is placed on his shoulders on the day he is born, just as sure as the bee and the cobra are the symbols of the Northlands.*

His mother's face beams with delight at the success of her match-making efforts. She had always held lofty hopes of marrying her son into a well-to-do family, so as to gain for him a firm foothold into higher society, and maybe even into the royal house. In her eyes, Keki's daughter fit that role perfectly.

Thut-nefer now realizes that he has been trapped in a net, like so many ibises, and he begins to feel a little squeamish.

Taking a quick gulp of wine, which now tastes very sour, indeed, he squeezes the frog amulet in his hand even harder.

He then ventures a quick look over to his friends, in search of their support, only to find them mingling with the musicians.

"Mind you, o' Keki, I was going to send him to the Temple of Userkaf as time-keeper to follow in his brother's footsteps; but now that you've laid claim to him, he is most honoured to serve under you," Perneb exclaims, between sips of wine.

And that is the end of that, Thut-nefer concludes to himself. *My fate is now sealed in a basalt sarcophagus for eternity, and only Atum can now intercede.*

Thut-nefer gets up slowly, looking to his uncle for permission to leave the table. His uncle nods at him and waves him off.

"Sheshu, there was some kind of commotion at the Temple of Ptah," he adds as an afterthought. "Apparently, it involved a scribe and a priest . . . unrest of sorts. Your mother mentioned you were at the Temple today with offerings. Did you see anything?" he inquires suspiciously.

Not waiting for an answer, he rambles on, "The governor has eyes and ears everywhere, and no one can escape his wrath. Be very careful, my boy.

See, I have told you the best of my inmost thoughts, which you should set steadfastly before your face. Now go, and enjoy the music with your friends."

In the background, the rhythms of the drums are beginning to work up to a steady crescendo.

Memi is clapping his hands vigorously, amongst the girls, relishing every moment. Ibeby is sitting at the table alone, watching the spectacle, sipping at his jug of beer.

Thut-nefer joins him and hands him the amulet discreetly.

"Keep it, to remember," he offers simply, raising his voice above the din of the drums.

"You would make a good priest in the order of Serqet. Quiet and steady, you are ready to sting at any given moment, attracting the poison towards you naturally. I've taken a liking to you, young Sesh. You are generous and pure of heart.

I would like to impart some knowledge, when you are ready to receive it. Memi tells me that you are mummifying ibises secretly to sell to the pilgrims."

Thut-nefer sits up in alarm and looks deeply into Ibeby's eyes. The younger man's hostility is well apparent.

"No, don't be afraid. Your secret will lay deep in the well of my heart. Save your poison for those who are deserving of it. You never cease to astonish me, and that's why I respected you from the moment we met at the Temple."

Thut-nefer shudders for a moment, and eases his gaze back to the musicians.

"I, too, have taken a liking to you, o' priest of Serqet, and as of today, we will seal our friendship by the token of this amulet. This frog and this lotus."

He snaps off a lotus bud from the collar around his neck and lays it on the table next to the small, exquisitely crafted amulet. Ibeby nods his head in acceptance, and puts his hand on Thut-nefer's shoulder, giving it a reassuring squeeze.

*   *   *

Chapter 11

Thut-nefer clutches the back of his neck with both hands and leans his head back toward the ceiling. "I feel groggy this morning," he groans to himself, "probably due to this headache that's pestering me."

He can hear his mother's muffled voice calling him to breakfast. The thought of eating, though, makes him wince.

"I must try and get some food down, as it will be a long and tiring day today," he senses, as he springs out of bed half-heartedly.

Thut-nefer downs a small cup of lemon juice sweetened with honey, which has a subtle, yet immediate effect on his headache.

Feeling somewhat better, he tears apart a stuffed pigeon from the preceding day's banquet, and slowly chews on the succulent, tender and well spiced meat.

Meryt-ra sits down next to him and places two loaves of fresh bread and a lettuce in front of him. She takes a small bite of lemon and then squeezes the juice onto the lettuce.

"Eat the lettuce. It will revive you," she encourages gently.

Thut-nefer looks up at her thankfully. "Aren't you going to eat with me?"

"No, I'll eat later, once I've finished my chores. Your uncle Perneb mentioned something about a land ownership deed of your father's. Did he not tell you? The governor wants to see it. It seems he's interested in a certain plot of land."

She pauses for a moment eyeing the lettuce hungrily, but then decides against it.

"That man is too greedy for his own good. It is part of the proper ways of the world, of Maat, that a man should follow in his father's footsteps, inheriting his social position, profession and property," she confides.

Then as an afterthought, she whispers discreetly. "That governor is a usurper of other people's lands and rights; soon he'll have more resources than our King."

Thut-nefer looks at his mother incredulously. Deep down, he knows she resents the injustice of the day, and longs for a time when Maat is neither neglected nor abused.

"Yes, Mother," he finds himself answering politely.

"I'll look for the title-deed," he adds with a grimace. "Well, what if I don't find it? What happens then?"

"He'll never leave you be, until he gets what he wants," she warns him sternly, as if that should end the conversation.

"May Serqet punish him with her burning wrath," Thut-nefer proclaims forcefully, "tightening his throat with a scorpion sting! That's how she treats the unrighteous[59]. O' Atum, have mercy on us!".

---

[59] Scorpion stings lead to paralysis, and Serqet's name describes this, as it means *(one who) tightens the throat*. However, Serqet's name can also be read as meaning *(one who) causes the throat to breathe*, and so, as well as being seen as stinging the unrighteous, Serqet was also seen as one who could cure.

"Yes, so true! May Atum give us strength of heart that we may overcome the evil that blocks our path!" Meryt-ra replies, as she looks at her son quizzically.

She then adds warily, "Sheshu, you're beginning to sound like a priest of Serqet."

*   *   *

The sun shines clear and bright over the horizon, casting its healing rays over the land of Kemet. After its long and hazardous journey through the underworld, it reemerges rejuvenated, bringing with it the hopes and strengths of a new day.

Thut-nefer steps out of the house and walks to the stables to load up his donkey. He takes a deep breath of the fresh, crisp, morning air.

Outside the stables, Meryt-mi-hapi and the stable boy greet him affectionately.

The boy steadies the donkey, while Thut-nefer places his equipment in the basket on its back, except for the sceptre, which he holds in his hand.

Meryt-mi-hapi loads two hin[60] jugs of beer, a small palm leaf basket, and two large loaves of bread onto the back of the donkey.

"Your lunch, o' Sesh," she nods, her eyes focusing on his face.

"You look better today, boy," he comments, squinting in the morning glare, trying to catch a glimpse of his wound.

The boy adores the attention, and without being told, dashes off to open the old wooden gate, the dog yelping at his heels.

Thut-nefer looks at Meryt-mi-hapi, her dark brown skin reflecting the morning's first light, causing him to pulsate.

---

[60]   Liquid measure

"You stay here with Meryt-ra. You'll be safe here as part of my household, until I can find your brother. I gave him my word that I would take care of you in his absence.

The only news I have so far is that he has joined a khen-khen ship sailing to the southlands. I'll be back by sunset; and hopefully I'll have more news by then."

"May Ptah refresh your heart through life and very old age," she calls out after him, as Thut-nefer pulls the donkey out of the old, worn out gate and briskly walks down the well trodden path towards Memi's family residence.

Flanked by two fields of flax, the path meanders towards the outer boundary stone. Thut-nefer pauses momentarily to admire the growing flax plants and bends down to retrieve a handful of soil, checking for its moisture.

Satisfied all is well, he moves onto the public thoroughfare, leaving behind his family property.

Further down the dusty road, by another large stone gate leading to Memi's residence, Thut-nefer halts abruptly. A young boy in his tattered kilt stands by the side of the road, weeping and sniveling, holding his right hand over his eye.

Desperately, he looks around for his mother. At last, he spots her sitting cross-legged just inside the stone gate, breast-feeding a young infant. Happily, he runs to her and plops himself down next to her.

She removes his hand and inspects his eye tenderly. Not uttering a word, she places the boy's head on her lap, and gently squeezes one of her breasts. A few drops of milk drip into his eye. The boy rubs his eye and stops crying.

Once again, having restored the morning calm, the woman continues to feed her infant.

Leaning heavily on his donkey, Thut-nefer decides to wait for his friend here, by the side of the road. He watches the woman and her children with interest.

"Oh, there you are, Sheshu," he hears Memi calling, as he walks towards his friend.

Memi quickly piles his belongings onto the donkey's back, in preparation to set out for their prescribed duty at the sun temple.

"A pilot who sees into the distance will not let his ship capsize [61]"

Thut-nefer murmurs to himself, casting a quick, furtive glance at the woman fondling her two children with great love.

"What was that you just said?" Memi asks Thut-nefer, adjusting his reed sandals for the long march ahead.

"Nothing, just a thought. Come now, we better get a move on."

Thut-nefer tugs at the reluctant donkey, which is busily sniffing the ground, in search of something to eat. The two scribes fall in, side by side, and pick up their pace.

"Shall we take the path along the edge of the valley to the sun temple, Sheshu?" Memi asks, gently nudging him in the back.

"Yes, fine, it'll get us there quicker," Thut-nefer answers, eagerly pulling the rope tied around his donkey's neck.

"Have you ever been to the sun temple?" Memi asks. "You know, they are just like pyramid complexes."

Thut-nefer shakes his head hastily, hoping to dislodge a fly that has been pestering him for some time.

Memi continues, "These sun temples have their own agricultural land, receive donations on festival days, and have their own temple personnel."

Bored by Memi's lecture, Thut-nefer shoves his friend playfully, causing him to stumble.

"The delight of Ra!" Thut-nefer's shrill voice blares out. "That's what the priests call the temple!"

---

[61]   Instructions of Amenemope

*   *   *

The sun temple, a huge obelisk like masonry structure perched high upon a red granite pedestal, looms above a sea of palms.

The two young scribes stand before this breathtaking sight in awe, as they approach the valley temple. Their eyes follow the magnificent lines of the temple, beginning with a colossal gateway and a pillared entrance, complete with four grand palm columns.

They watch dozens of priests clad in pure white linens carry their offerings and make their way up the monumental causeway that extends to the upper temple, which is built upon a natural platform of rock along the edge of the desert.

Near the valley temple, on open land, the shrill, deafening cries of the cattle herders can be heard, men desperately trying to keep their unruly animals in line.

A cloud of dust from the tumult on the ground looms heavy in the air, eerily blurring the sun's rays, like a fast approaching sandstorm.

Thut-nefer and Memi decide to take a moment to pause and adjust their clothing, as they would soon be in the midst of this chaos.

Memi pulls out the water jug and hands it to Thut-nefer, who takes a sip. He pours a little into his hand and rubs his face and eyes before handing it back.

"You know, Sheshu, Khentiki has been relieved of his post at school," Memi states between two mouthfuls, dramatically spitting out the latter.

"Direct order from the governor," he continues. "I heard it from my father. He reckons that he'll be moved to a position where he won't have that much sway on the young minds of the day."

"Yes, that would make sense," Thut-nefer mumbles, trying to remove a small pebble stuck between his foot and his sandal.

"That's another tactic on the part of the governor to influence the new generation of scribes towards his own interests. Another form of deceit—feed them the knowledge he wants them to know, and then bury the rest that contravenes his interest."

"That'll make them no better than the cattle out there," Memi asserts, adjusting his wig carefully, while waiting for Thut-nefer.

"That's just it, Memi, my friend. The young bud of a lotus plant has the light captured in its very essence, even before it reaches the surface."

"Just like the fabric of our own soul . . . Servant in the Place of Truth! Khentiki's new title!" Memi adds.

Thut-nefer looks at Memi with an expression of disgust, and leads the way towards the valley temple.

Weaving through groups of cattle and men, they keep a watchful eye for flying beasts' tails. The two young scribes make their way to a raised wooden platform with four colourfully painted columns and a roof.

Under the roof, painted in different shades of blue, a young priest beckons, inviting them up to its hospitable shade. He welcomes the duo warmly, as they clamber up the wooden ladder, and points to a new reed mat, designating their appointed places to sit.

Today, they would be counting the herd of the temple and those of the surrounding area. Thut-nefer looks around, inspecting the cattle, while undoing the scrolls of papyrus and arranging them numerically on the reed mat in front of him.

Two old wooden chairs stand side by side, and a three-legged table, well-stocked with four earthenware jugs of beer, obviously intended for the head priest and the supervisor of scribes.

The head herder approaches, then stands silently, waiting for permission to speak. Thut-nefer removes the reed pen from between his teeth and stares down at him hard.

"Greetings, herder. Have your men line up the cattle in rows of five. Neat rows . . . you know the procedure."

"Yes, o' Sesh," he acknowledges pleasantly, hoping to appease the scribe. He turns around and looks at his men gruffly, holding a coil of rope in one hand, while raising the other.

He shouts, "Neat rows of five! Any man who breaks the ranks will be tied to the stake and beaten!"

Memi's writing tablet is neatly tucked under his arm and a basket-work cylindrical container for the papyrus scrolls rests by his feet. He gazes around and watches men and beast line up.

Memi nudges Thut-nefer with his foot. "Look, Sheshu," he nods, pointing discreetly with his head in the direction of an approaching figure. "Oh no, it can't be . . . it's Kheruef! Quick, get up on your feet!" Memi whispers, horrified.

Thut-nefer gets up reluctantly, just in time to meet the arriving supervisor and his two young aides, who eagerly trot close behind.

With great pomp, Kheruef signals his two young attendants to help him up the wooden ladder. Once up on the stage, he condescendingly looks down at Thut-nefer and Memi, while his two aides dust him down.

A layer of dust had accumulated and settled on his wig, causing him to sneeze. His pot belly protrudes over his kilt, which is woven from the finest of linen, reserved for high ranking officials only. It shakes and then trembles, while he adjusts the large turquoise necklace around his neck.

He settles himself down on one of the chairs and greedily helps himself to one of the beer jugs.

Thut-nefer can tell that, by his actions and looks, this man has been bought by the governor. *Like a royal seal stuck on a wine jar, corruption is stamped all over him*, he thinks to himself.

The scribe takes an immediate disliking to Khuruef, the supervisor, who begins to sweat at the brow, even though he is sitting in the shade.

"Another sign of the wealthy's soft living in times of others' hunger and strife," Thut-nefer mutters under his breath to Memi.

Thut-nefer's thoughts turn toward the truth of what he sees before him. *When the Great River refuses to give its abundant waters, greed is like an illness flowing through the internal rivers of the body, preventing the life-giving floods.*

Isfet[62] is on the rise, just like this man's pot belly quivering with every gluttonous gulp of beer, originally intended as an offering by some poor wretch, in dire hope of salvation.

The identification of Maat with the will of the King has broken up. No longer in control of his bark, he is floating helplessly at the mercy of the river, only to fragment once he hits the cataract.

And who better than these riverbank rats to feast on the state of affairs.

Thut-nefer recalls an ancient prophecy and sees the seeds of it taking shape, even now. *'This land is in commotion, and no one knows what the result may be, for it is hidden from speech, sight, and hearing because of dullness, silence being to the fore.*[63]'

The head priest is ushered in by two helpers, and he takes his place on the empty wooden chair next to the supervisor.

They exchange greetings politely, and Thut-nefer can tell there has been no love lost between them.

---

[62] chaos

[63] Prophecy of Neferty

The priest nods at Thut-nefer, who immediately lowers his head with respect. His fresh, white linen robe is spotless, with no sign of accumulated dust.

Thut-nefer stares for a moment at his freshly shaven head, which reflects the light, like the water of a sacred lake shimmering in the morning sun. The simple reed sandals on his feet are newly made, and contribute to his general appearance of cleanliness.

This priest, muses Thut-nefer, *is a rather thin man, but nonetheless sinewy. His dark eyes portray a fortitude of faith and a determination to conclude whatever business he sets for himself.*

The herdsman, upon seeing the head priest, begins to chant.

"Come on, get away! Do not speak in the presence of the praised one! He detests people talking. He does what is right. He will not ignore any complaint. Pass on in quiet and in order!"

The priest looks over at the herdsman and gives him the order to proceed, by extending his hand.

The supervisor grunts and takes a quick gulp from the earthenware jug, oblivious to the crassness of his action. For him, the end result of the count would be whatever number the governor had dictated.

The cattle begin to move past the shelter in neat rows of fives, each herder tending to his prescribed animals with ultimate care and devotion.

Thut-nefer and Memi carefully count each row separately, occasionally cross-checking their numbers while writing them down. The air is heavily laden with dust and sand churned up by the hooves of each passing row of animals.

Thut-nefer's eyes begin to itch and his throat is parched, like one of the papyrus scrolls laid out in front of him.

He looks at his friend compassionately. A layer of sand has covered his wig and face, and only his eyes can be seen through the mask, appearing as if he had just stepped out of an intense sandstorm.

The sun had passed its zenith by several hours, as the herdsmen bring in the last row of cattle.

The head herdsman follows closely behind, holding up his coil of rope, signaling the end of the cattle count.

Thut-nefer looks up, relieved; trying to rub his throbbing eyes.

Memi quickly inserts two new cakes of ink in both their palettes, moistening them with his wet brush. He dusts the papyrus scrolls and arranges them in front of his friend for the final tally.

Thut-nefer stands up, attempting to get the circulation moving in his legs again, as they had cramped from his protracted sitting.

The dust finally begins to settle, and the rays of the sun begin to eat their way through the opaqueness, like a caterpillar gnawing at a leaf.

The supervisor, now visibly impatient, grunts at the young scribe.

"Come now! You, there, hurry up and finish!"

Thut-nefer, determined to complete his work in an orderly fashion, ignores him, thankfully accepting a jug of water from one of the young priests.

The cool water revives him again. He passes it on to Memi, who takes a long deep drink of the refreshing water. Gratefully handing it back to the priest, he busies himself with checking the final tally.

The supervisor, furious with the delay, raises his guttural voice, "Finish your work, scribes, or you'll have me to deal with! I'll skin you alive!"

The head priest signals the young priest to retire, quietly concerned the supervisor will follow through with his threat and punish the two scribes.

Thut-nefer understands the gesture and gets to work making a final copy for the supervisor to take with him.

By mid-afternoon, Thut-nefer and Memi have finished their work.

Once having completed their task, one of the young priests appears at their side, there to fetch them to wash up and enjoy a simple meal of bread, white cheese, cucumbers, radishes and a little honey . . . *with* the head priest.

The two scribes follow the priest into the shade of the first courtyard, just inside the valley temple, where they sit down on a clean reed mat laid out for them.

Thut-nefer can feel the peace and serenity of the atmosphere affecting his brittle, dry nerves. The muscles in his body begin to relax and he starts eating slowly with great relish.

"Aren't you going to join us?" Memi asks the young priest standing next to him.

"No," he answers with a pleasant smile. "We eat later, once we've finished our duties."

"Sounds like you have a very busy time ahead," Thut-nefer interrupts.

"Yes," the young priest replies "the cattle count has upset our routine. After eating, we will wash ourselves down with natron and then we'll be bathing in the sacred lake for the third time today. Let alone shaving all the hair off our bodies. And all that just to be ready for duties at the temple," he confesses humbly.

"Purity certainly involves complicated ablutions!" Memi joins in, laughing jovially between mouthfuls.

This priest's simple innocence, Thut-nefer ponders, *is truly refreshing.*

"Ah, yes, the head priest wishes to thank you for a job well done. He would have come to thank you personally, but he is busy purifying himself for his sunset duties up in the temple.[64] He also wishes you to have a little of this myrrh incense, as a sign of gratitude."

The young priest produces two small linen packets of incense balls and hands them over to each scribe.

"Please convey to the Pure One that it is our honor to serve under him," Thut-nefer replies politely, his nostrils twitching at the blissful scent escaping from the packets in his hand.

*   *   *

---

[64] From such purificatory rites the priests were often times known as the "pure ones" regardless of status within the temples

Chapter 12

Feeling exhausted, the two scribes decide to take a shortcut through the temple lands, knowing it will eventually lead them to the main pathway, just outside the outskirts of Men-nefer. Not far from the main thoroughfare, they decide to rest under a lone Nahyet tree.[65]

Thut-nefer can hear the cracking of slingshots and the whiz of mud projectiles flying overhead. Regardless of the adolescent play of local boys, Thut-nefer gazes across the horizon and notices the wheat and barley fields, looking their best in the golden, late afternoon glow.

He breathes a deep sigh and pauses a few moments.

The wheat, heavily laden with fully mature husks, sways slightly in the gentle breeze, like a pregnant woman ambling along, slowly from side to side.

"It's a pleasing sight, my dear Memi," he comments softly, apprehensive he might lose the calming effect of his vision.

"Yes, indeed, my dear friend," Memi answers, sitting with his back against the tree while holding onto the donkey. "It'll be harvest soon."

---

[65]   Ficus sycamoros

Thut-nefer half closes his eyes and watches the wheat dance in the breeze, allowing his soul to revive again.

"The truth that makes alive," he murmurs to himself, unawares, surprised at the resonance of his own voice, as if it were coming from another realm.

All of a sudden out of the blue an image manifests itself in his mind's eye. He can clearly make out the face of Khuruef, the supervisor, scowling.

It is obvious he is in great pain, the scribe acknowledges to himself.

This man has fed his belly with fire, contradicting all teachings. It is his soul crying out in desperation. No amount of wealth can assuage that inner pain. If only he knew!

Thut-nefer opens his eyes and lets out a shudder of relief, appreciative he walks in his own sandals, not those of this or any other man.

The heart goes blind, say the wise, *stone upon stone, until it is entombed for near eternity, ready to be gobbled up by Ammit.*

Could it be that Ibeby is secretly trying to teach me the ways of Serqet? he wonders to himself. *He is so near and yet so far!*

Memi, taking in the natural beauty of the moment a few cubits away, feels compelled to break into a recital.

Thut-nefer, coming to from his daydreams, listens intently to Memi's gentle voice, swaying like the wheat in the dry north wind.

"The young sycamore that you have planted with your hand has grown and has begun to speak sweet words, like drops of honey.

She is slender and her branch beautiful and green as papyrus, and she is laden with food that rivals the redness of rubies.

The air under her is moist and fresh, so come and spend time in the garden.

The gardeners are happy and rejoicing in seeing you and bring you different bread, flowers and fresh fruit.

So come and enjoy this day, sitting under the shade, and I will keep the secret and I will not mention anything I see.[66]"

The sound of hoof beats and the cough of a man infiltrate Thut-nefer's conscious mind. He reluctantly slides back to reality.

"Who goes there?" he hears Memi calling to the approaching stranger.

"It is I, trader of mats from among the papyrus-gatherers of the marshlands. My mats are of the best quality, stitched with linen thread, soft and comfortable, even to the most aching bodies!"

Thut-nefer could not place the man's accent, which somehow seemed foreign to him.

"Step forward, trader," Memi counters. "You are in the presence of scribes of the holy city of Men-nefer."

The short man steps forward, pulling a donkey heavily laden with mats, and respectfully stops a short distance away.

"Greetings, o' scribes of the Holy City; you wish to inspect my mats? I'm on my way to the market. I can offer you a mat at a very reasonable rate," the man ventures boldly, breathing heavily, as if it was him who was carrying the mats and not the donkey.

"We wish no mats, trader," Memi replies suspiciously. "You are on temple lands. Why are you not using the public path?"

"It seems I've taken a wrong turn somewhere. Please forgive my ignorance."

Thut-nefer can see that this man is nobody's fool. His eyes, buried deep in his frizzy hair, which is tied back by a rawhide head band, give him away almost immediately.

---

[66] Poem translated by Maspero

The man's kilt, not of the usual white linen, is made of a coloured material, tightly wrapped around his waist. His sandals are strapped to his belt.

"You better turn around and follow the irrigation ditch you just passed a ways back. It'll take you right to the public path, wandering stranger. Hurry up before the priests catch you; otherwise, you might end up in deep trouble!"

Thut-nefer directs the stranger silently with his arm, as he watches him disappear hastily amongst the swaying wheat.

Memi spits out the nearly ripe wheat seeds he had just popped into his mouth moments before.

"Almost ripe," he decides and then quickly adds "You gave him a fright, Sheshu! Do not worry about him, for the Asiatic is a crocodile on his riverbank. He snatches a lonely serf, but he will never rob in the vicinity of a populous town.[67]"

The two scribes look at each other and smile. Tired, but satisfied they resume their walk back. The sun is sinking into the underworld, leaving its last blaze of light to humanity to remember it by.

Quickening their pace in the hope of reaching home before it gets dark, they decide to cut through the artisan's quarters. The two young scribes disappear into the narrow maze of small alleyways, making their way carefully, sticking close together.

A group of young children, appearing from nowhere, follow them chanting and laughing.

One boy, breaking away from the others, walks up to Thut-nefer and offers his services, in the hope of earning whatever tidbit he can lay his hands on. The poverty and hunger is apparent in his dull and glazed eyes.

Thut-nefer waves the boy away with his sceptre.

---

[67] The Prophecy of Neferty

Begging for something to eat, the children a few steps behind begin to pull at Memi with their grubby hands.

Thut-nefer, no longer able to brush off the pleading children, reaches in the basket dangling from the donkey's back and retrieves the last loaf of bread and a few remaining cucumbers.

He hands them to the boy silently, watching his eyes light up in gratitude.

Leaving the children to squabble over their bounty, the two scribes quickly vanish around the next corner.

Thut-nefer looks up and down the side street, half expecting to see the usual welcoming committee of hungry children, but sees no one.

Relieved, they step out onto the major thoroughfare, not far from the stone gate leading to Memi's residence.

Content to be back after a long tiring day, Memi asks, "Won't you come in, Sheshu?" insisting on inviting his friend in for a meal.

Thut-nefer refuses bluntly, citing his fatigue as an excuse.

Leaving Memi behind, standing by the large stone gate, Thut-nefer slowly trundles on home.

*   *   *

Thut-nefer raps on the old wooden door with his sceptre. His donkey snorts loudly and stomps its right front hoof, sensing its stable close by. Impatiently, Thut-nefer bangs on the door again.

A young boy opens the ancient door with a great smile on his face, happy to see his beloved master. Within moments, though, his smile fades away, as he anxiously recalls the bad news he has to report.

Not able to contain himself, he discloses the bad tidings to his master—some of the bee hives had been broken into, and a good quantity of honey combs had been taken from the hives.

Many of the cylindrical hives made of dried mud had been damaged, especially the detachable section at the back, which is used for harvesting the honey combs.

They were no longer stacked neatly in horizontal rows, having been plundered by shameless men who knew what they were doing.

Burned, dried cow dung, used to smoke the bees out, was scattered all over the ground in a dire attempt to snatch the precious nectar from the ravaging bees.

The boy is in tears, as he concludes his sad report. Unable to look at his master, he fidgets with his hands, staring at the ground. Thut-nefer is furious at the perpetrators and their unrighteous actions, yet feels compassion for the young boy, while he leads him and the donkey to the stables.

An unusual quiet settles in among the household, as darkness overcomes the fading light.

"Ra wept and his tears fell to the ground and were turned into bees."

Thut-nefer looks at the boy and clears his throat to continue. By now everyone was listening attentively, and they all knew the wisdom of their master.

"The bees, then, began to build their honeycombs and became very active on every kind of flower belonging to the plant kingdom. Thus wax came into being, and thus was honey created from the tears of Ra."

A general sigh of relief could be heard coming from the kitchen, as the womenfolk unburden their heavy hearts.

Like a hunter's powerful arrow piercing the heart of his quarry, Thut-nefer's words, had struck the right chord, alleviating their anguish caused by the devastating theft of their hives.

He orders the boy to light a small fire and shouts to the women in the kitchen that he would be having his meal out in the open.

From where he stood, Thut-nefer could hear their happy giggles and their mischievous whisperings that their master would be dining with them.

"Fetch me your father, boy, and a jug of beer from the mistress of the house. No one can steal the tears of Ra and walk away unscathed."

*   *   *

The croaking sound of the frogs welcome the darkness, as it envelopes the world in a dark shroud.

The flickering of the fire and the flames' dance illuminates the sullen faces of the household. The buzz of the mosquitoes, as they descend on their victims, is intolerable, but is drowned out by the eerie calls of the Thicknee.

The night's awakening calls forth the senses of each man, woman and child.

Thut-nefer raises the earthen jug to his lips and takes a long, deep draw, washing down his meal of the leftovers from the prior day's banquet.

Meryt-ra is sitting next to him, silently waiting for her son to conduct their affairs. He retrieves a few hot coals from the fire with his sceptre, picks them up with his bare hands and quickly throws them into an empty mud tray.

He slowly unties the linen packet of myrrh and takes out an incense ball, placing it delicately on the hot coals. The wonderfully aromatic scent of the myrrh engulfs his nostrils, leaving him transfixed, unable to move.

His eyes dilate with ecstasy, as he momentarily drifts away from any semblance of concern for those awaiting on him.

Eventually, Thut-nefer returns from his reverie and breaks the silence.

"Listen to the wisdom of the men of old," he announces, raising his voice above the din of the serenading frogs.

"Serve God, that he may do the like for you, with offerings for replenishing the altars and with carving; it is that which will show forth your name . . . and God is aware of whoever serves Him.

Provide for men the cattle of God, for He made heaven and earth at their desire. He suppressed the greed of the waters;

He gave the breath of life to their noses, for they are likenesses of Him which issued from His flesh.

He shines in the sky for the benefit of their hearts; He has made herbs, cattle, and fish to nourish them.

He has killed His enemies and destroyed His own children, because they had planned to make rebellion;

He makes daylight for the benefit of their hearts, and he sails around the sea in order to see them. He has raised up a shrine behind them, and when they weep, He hears.

He has made them rulers even from the egg, a lifter to lift the load from the back of the weak man. He has made for them magic, to be into weapons, to ward off what may happen.

Be watchful over it by night, as by day. How has He killed the disaffected! Even as a man strikes his son for his brother's sake, for God knows every name.[68]"

Thut-nefer remains silent for a while, letting his words sink in. He looks at the members of his household, all crowded around the fire, looking up at him in wonder.

The young children are quietly playing a game with stones, flicking one into the air, while quickly collecting the remaining stones on the ground.

---

[68]   Teachings of Merikare

"I have passed my judgment as a scribe of the holy city," he concludes gravely.

He pauses for a moment to recollect his thoughts, while watching the children deeply absorbed in their game.

"We have to hold in check the rivalry of these nobles, who wish to retard our prosperity for the sake of their own.

You have to disappear to reappear. Just as they disappeared with our honey, we will reappear with theirs, but without hurting the beauty of creation and without them knowing.

We shall prepare our magic well and will strike when we are ready. Until then we are all committed to secrecy. We must be more attentive in guarding our property, and everybody big and small must play their part.

What gets stolen from us is less for us to eat. We live in hard times, where famines are common and every little bit counts. Just as the white heron fishes for fish and frogs along the canal, waiting to strike with its pointed beak, we too shall wait and strike.

The footprints of these wretched thieves only mark where they were. You, Overseer, under cover of darkness, will follow their tracks while they are fresh.

Take the dog and report back as soon as you find out anything. Stay in the shadows and don't confront anyone. Remember, Overseer, that the hunters of the marshes show a tame bird to attract other waterfowl."

At last, in the sanctuary of the living quarters, Thut-nefer stretches out his tired body on a comfortable mat, pulling out a pillow to lean on.

The half finished game of senet lies between him and Meryt-ra. Sleepiness is overpowering his resistance to stay awake. His mother begins to prepare his bed, seeing her son exhausted.

Thut-nefer drags himself across the room and throws himself on the bed. Meryt-ra hands her son a clean linen sheet, which he uses to cover his whole body and head protecting him from the famished mosquitoes buzzing around him.

"Good night, Mother" he manages to croak from under the sheet.

"Good night, my son," she answers softly.

*   *   *

Chapter 13

Shrill screams and the dog's bark wake Thut-nefer up with a start. He rushes to the window to see the boy loading up his slingshot and shouting at the top of his voice. The dog is rushing around in circles, barking wildly.

"The bee-eaters are here. Fly away and find your food elsewhere!" the boy shouts in his high-pitched voice, amidst the crack of his sling.

Thut-nefer looks up into the sky and sees a flock of bee-eaters circling above the beehives. Their bright blue and green feathers sparkle in the first light, as they fly high above and then swoop down at breakneck speed, mastering their turns with great agility.

He dresses quickly and rushes down to help scare the birds off, colliding with Meryt-mi-hapi at the door leading to the garden.

"You're already up, Sesh. Your mother sent me to wake you and tell you to come and have your morning meal."

"Good, good. Come now, let's go and help the boy with the bee-eaters first."

Clapping their hands loudly, they both walk towards the far end of the garden, where the cylindrical mud hives are stacked.

By the pond Thut-nefer, stops momentarily, bends down and inhales deeply the wonderful aroma of the blue lotus, already in full bloom. He can feel his eyes dilate, as the scent clears his nostrils and penetrates deep into his lungs.

"To assume the form of a blue lotus," he mutters quietly, "I am a pure lotus, coming forth as the god of light, keeper of the nose of Ra, and keeper of the head of Hathor.

That, which I do, that which I come down for, I seek it for Horus. I am pure, coming forth from the field.[69]"

As he stands up, he feels a slight dizziness, which he shrugs off instantly, his eyes falling onto the smiling Meryt-mi-hapi. Her eyes shine like the most polished basalt of old.

"Come on, girl, clap your hands," he orders lamely, unable to hide from her laughing eyes.

Famished, Thut-nefer sits down at the low table and heartily attacks the breakfast his mother had prepared: bean paste fried in oil, salted, aged white cheese, fresh cucumber and lettuce with a sprig of lemon juice, and a large bowl of milk boiled with whole wheat and dates.

"The overseer wishes to speak to you," Meryt-ra whispers to her son.

"Let him approach and give him his breakfast," Thut-nefer gasps out loud for all to hear.

He throws a piece of bread to the dog, who wags its tail in hope that it, too, would get something to eat.

"What have you got to report, o' Overseer of the Lands?"

"It seems they were expecting me; for no sooner had I shown myself on their land, I found myself surrounded. They took me in and I had to wait some time before the overseer came to talk to me.

---

[69]   Papyrus of Ani

There, in the middle of the courtyard, they had tied up an Asiatic. He was bound by the feet and the arms to a stake. Obviously, he had been beaten on the back in the usual manner.

The marks on his back were agonizing to look at, even to the most ruthless of beings.

The man kept whining unintelligible words, some in our language and some in his.

At long last, I could just make out what he was saying: 'Behold, it was the sweetness which seduced me to do it'[70]"

Shendwa takes a moment to study his master's face. Drawing a blank he continues with his report.

"He keeps repeating this over and over, as if they had drummed it into his poor head, like the priests of ptah teaching their disciples their lessons."

Thut-nefer interrupts the overseer briefly, now looking annoyed.

"They're covering up their tracks."

Anger begins to show on his face, a tightening constriction of his jaw and a glowering in his eyes. Shendwa knows his master only too well and falls silent, waiting for the approaching storm.

"It takes more than one man to do all that damage!" he shouts at the overseer.

"Yes, master," the overseer manages to croak meekly, preferring to ride out the storm.

"This better not happen again, overseer; otherwise it'll be the stake for you. Injustice cannot be cured by injustice, but you must realize the seriousness of these circumstances!"

"Yes, o' wise Sesh. No man shall enter these lands, except over my dead body," he decrees sternly with more confidence, feeling that he had weathered out the eye of the storm.

---

[70] Briefe aus Illahun => London pUC 32124 => Brief eines Dieners der Stiftung über Honig

"Good, good, overseer, now listen well to the wisdom of the men of old, and remember to . . ." Thut-nefer now calming down slightly, clears his throat.

"Do justice that you may live long upon earth. Calm the weeper; do not oppress the widow; do not oust a man from his father's property.

Do not put your trust in length of years, for they regard a lifetime as an hour. A man survives after death, and his deeds are laid before him in a heap.

Existence yonder is eternal, and he who complains of it is a fool; but as for him who attains it, he will be like a god yonder, striding forward like the lords of eternity.[71]"

Thut-nefer gazes at the overseer. Looking to see if his words had sunk in, he focuses sharply on the man's eyes.

"Come Shendwa, walk with me to the ferry. We'll take the shortcut through the fields," Thut-nefer commands, as he stands up and stretches his legs, ready to depart.

"I want to check the cucumbers growing in the southernmost field. It's on our way. The crows have devastated it so badly, I've sent the boy out with his sling to try to kill one."

Thut-nefer feels the morning cobwebs in his mind's eye begin to fade, as they walk single file along the narrow path. He pauses for a moment and takes off his sandals, preferring to continue barefoot along the edge of the muddy irrigation ditch.

He hears the boy calling from a short distance away, as he proudly waves a dead crow above his head. Thut-nefer laughs loudly. Pointing, he calls out to the overseer.

"Look! The young rascal has managed to kill one!"

Shendwa stops by a young palm tree and cuts off a couple of branches using his sharp flint knife. He strips off the thin

---

[71]   Teachings of Merikare

long leaves from the branches and quickly ties the two branches together in the form of a cross.

He zigzags through the cucumber field, choosing a good spot to ram the branches into the soft earth. The boy proudly hands his father the dead bird, its limp neck dangling and flopping from side to side with each one of his movements.

"This sling is the best, o' Sesh!" he exclaims excitedly to his master.

Shendwa ties the dead crow to the palm branches and steps back to examine his work.

"This is good. That should keep them away. The crows are afraid of death!"

Thut-nefer raises his sceptre above his head, "Well done!" he proclaims solemnly to Shendwa.

His eyes, though, secretly wander over to the rest of the crows, which are watching the spectacle from a safe distance. *So death is what keeps the living apart,* he muses, sucking in the unnatural silence.

Suddenly, with perfect timing, all the crows commence squawking a horrific mantra, drowning out the lingering stillness.

"Mourn death, o crows!" Thut-nefer shouts at the black and grey birds, creating even more confusion.

"Shendwa, I must be on my way. I can see the ferry about to cross the canal," Thut-nefer calls out over the ruckus of the crows, as he quickly sets out, plodding his way through the muddy fields.

*   *   *

"You bless my ferry, o' Sesh, with your presence," the ferry-man groans, while steadying his craft with his long wooden pole. The scribe jumps on with poise.

"Take us across, o' ferry-man; I have no time to waste. The harvest is knocking at our gates and we have much to prepare."

The ferry-man nods his head, and pushes his pole deep into the water.

"Did the artisan pay you his dues? Thut-nefer asks. Not waiting for an answer, he rambles on. "You must show more mercy and compassion in your heart, ferry-man. My heart, my mother; my heart, my mother! My heart, whereby I came into being![72]"

The ferry-man looks sullen, thrusting his pole with force deep into the water again, hoping to reach the bank quickly. The bottom of the reed ferry scrapes the muddy bank and grinds to an abrupt halt.

Thut-nefer loses his balance for a split second. The ferry-man steadies him with his sinewy arm. Their eyes meet. The hardship of the times is well inscribed in his drawn face, like a fine chiseled stele of granite made by the best artisans of the southlands.

"My Sesh, the Priest of Serqet has left a message for you. He wishes to see you when it's convenient."

"I'm rather busy, but tell him I will meet him by the old willow when the sun is at its highest. Keep my words in your ears like golden earrings, that you may find peace, o' ferry-man."

He hands him a flat loaf of bread stuffed with fried bean paste.

"Now, sit down and eat," Thut-nefer urges the man gently, as he takes a deep breath and starts to scramble up the slippery embankment, occasionally leaning on his sceptre for balance.

---

[72]   The prayer of Ani

For a quick moment, he looks back, waves his sceptre, and vanishes over the top of the earthen levee.

*   *   *

When Thut-nefer arrives, the administrative buildings are a hive of activity. The arrangements for the harvest have begun.

Mobilizing the entire population of the city, women and children included, and the surrounding villages are no easy task.

It requires a highly organized, basic work force to keep all the pieces in place, even though the expected harvest seems to be poor.

Thut-nefer walks up to Memi, who is leaning against a giant pillar, waiting for his friend.

"Health and prosperity, Memi," Thut-nefer greets his friend casually from the corner of his mouth. "How come you're not running your errands?"

"Because, I'm always waiting for you," Memi retorts, lifting his sceptre in a mock blow.

"Come on, my son, let's go in," he adds sarcastically.

They both move towards the entrance, weaving through the crowds of young scribes, into the main court-yard, past the large statue of Ptah holding his customary three scepters: the was, the djed and the ankh.

In the far corner of the large hall, they spot their superintendent, a short and stout man who sits cross-legged on a mat with a large pile of papyrus scrolls neatly stacked in front of him.

They approach him cautiously and greet him with respect. He summons them to sit down, before engaging in any speech.

He looks tired and frustrated, his beady little eyes shifting from one scribe to the other.

He retrieves two papyrus scrolls from the pile in front of him, reading out their names.

"You're Khentiki's scribes?"

They both nod silently. "You're also *the trouble-makers.* Just like your master."

The superintendent looks at them unsympathetically, his shifty beady eyes, now settling down on the pile of papyrus in front of him.

Thut-nefer gets up and stands still, shifting his balance from one foot to another, staring at the poorly woven mat. *It sounded as though even the Asiatic had better mats than this one,* he chuckles to himself.

After receiving his scroll, Memi stands up next to Thut-nefer, and both men remain waiting for the superintendent to give them leave.

"*Behold, he who once recorded the harvest now knows nothing about it, while he who never ploughed for himself, is now the owner of corn; the reaping takes place, but is not reported. The scribe sits in his office, but his hands are idle in it.*[73]"

Thut-nefer thinks to himself what Khentiki, the master, had always taught them and now he finds it so relevant, he can't help but stare at the superintendent in astonishment.

Search for truth and knowledge of the ancients, he mulls over, completely taken aback by reality, *in order to be able to pass on that knowledge to future generations.*

And now, they're branding him as a troublemaker. All keepers of knowledge are troublemakers, rebels of sorts, and once branded, it sticks like overripe figs; nobody wants to hear the truth.

"*Follow the way of the lotus and you shall not succumb!*"

---

[73]   Prophecies of Neferty

Yes, indeed, Thut-nefer recalls him lecturing clearly, as if it was yesterday.

The scribe had spent enough time listening to Khentiki to know that there was no easy route, no shortcut to true knowledge, nor to pass it on. He reflected further upon the master's words:

The soul comes to the place which it knows, and it will not overstep the ways of the past; no magic can oppose it, and it will reach to those who will give it water. Give me water. Water is knowledge. Bend down and drink, to your heart's content.

But beware of those who wish to deprive you of it and keep you in a constant state of thirst. For then, you are their slaves. Atum is brandishing his power through a small and frail flower, offering water and light. And Heket, the frog, patiently waits for the resurrection of all souls, croaking at night in the river and ponds of our beloved land.

After what seems an eternity, the shifty-eyed superintendent waves them off, without even sparing a glance.

The two scribes take their usual two steps back and turn around; then, they walk towards the entrance without speaking a word.

Thut-nefer sinks deeper and deeper into his thoughts with each step, as he heads towards the brilliant sunshine bursting through the main portal. Once outside, Memi breaks the silence and nudges his friend.

"Look, Sheshu, that old statue of Ptah! They never removed it when they rebuilt this part of the school."

Thut-nefer looks at the finely polished sculpture made of red granite standing by the entrance.

"Quite a sight, you're right." Thut-nefer grins. "There stands Ptah, unwavering in all his magnificence, basking in the morning light, watching the human element's frantic effort to organize itself to the highest degree. The first day of Shemu[74] is to burst on us, like the sun through that portal."

"Yes," Memi responds solemnly, "and with it comes the Djed Pillar festival, celebrating the symbol and its powers. It's so spiritually refreshing! And do you sense the excitement in the air?"

The two scribes fall silent, taking in the overriding sense of exhilaration they feel vibrating through their surroundings.

Memi chuckles and looks at his friend dubiously, "So, we're troublemakers."

Thut-nefer gives him a long, cold look, which stops Memi flat.

"Come on, Memi, let's sit in the shade of those columns over there, away from the noise."

Once settled, Memi unravels his papyrus and begins to read his duties. He quickly reads the date, "Peret[75], fourth month, 27th day. First cattle count in the reign of our King Qakara Ibi."

He falls silent as he reads. Thut-nefer's eyes wander over to the hustle-bustle, only to be briskly interrupted by his friend.

"Read your papyrus, Sheshu. It seems we've been assigned to the Tax assessors. O' Great Atum, have mercy on us."

He looks at his friend with a grieved look on his face. The tax assessors are the first teams of surveyors to inspect the ripening crops. They measure the fields to calculate the area under cultivation, which would then be compared to records of previous years.

Also, samples of the grain would be tested to judge the quality of the crop. An estimate would then be made of the

---

[74] Shemu: month of the harvest

[75] Peret: the coming forth of the land out of the inundation

expected yield. The collection of taxes was often performed by coercion.

Farmers owing taxes were either forced to hand over arrears on the spot, or brought before courts that dispensed summary justice. Memi knew as well as Thut-nefer: tax assessors were hated by the common populace.

He watches quietly as Thut-nefer unravels his papyrus slowly and reads:

"The superintendent of produce, who fixes the grain measure, who sets the grain tax amount for his lord, who registers the islands which appear as new land over the cartouche of His Majesty, And sets up the landmark at the boundary of the arable land, who protects the King by his tax rolls, And makes the Register of the Black land.

The scribe who places the divine offerings for all the gods, the donor of land grants to the people.[76]"

He pauses for a moment to draw his breath.

"There is no doubt that this is our punishment. They've given us marks of disfavor. Now, we're officially branded and under their surveillance. All our actions will be scrutinized, so we must be careful," he murmurs quietly to Memi.

He then continues to read from his papyrus:

"The royal Scribe, Pepi-nakht, orders you to join the tax collectors, henceforth, for the duration of the harvest."

Memi's face turns pale with grief. This was one post to which he never expected to be assigned. Thut-nefer sits quietly by, watching the ever increasing traffic of scribes.

It all seems to be one hectic mess. Disorganization is the heart of organization, he thinks.

He looks at his friend compassionately. "You know, a sage once recommended that If a poor cultivator is in arrears with

---

[76] Instructions of Amenope

his taxes, remit two-thirds of them[77]," Thut-nefer reminds him light-heartedly, hoping to comfort his friend.

Memi, not taken with his friend's dry humour, continues to sulk. "If we do that, rest assured, we're not going to end up in a good way."

"Yes, you're right. They'll cut both our hands off,[78] thinking that we're falsifying the records! There's no compassion left in the hearts; when in actual fact, all we're doing is following the wisdom of the ancients.

Did you not notice that the young scribes are not studying the ancient texts? They want the people to forget, so that they can introduce their new beliefs."

"Yes, *and* to fatten their stomachs," Memi grumbles. "Do away with masters like Khentiki, bury them alive! Who needs keepers of knowledge in our day?"

"Yes," counters Thut-nefer, "but a lotus flower, once it has bloomed for its three days, sinks into the water and turns into a pod. Once ripe, it bursts open, flinging out thousands of tiny seeds. Each seed has a small membrane attached to it, so that it can float with the current to an open space further down river.

Eventually, the membrane dissolves and the seed sinks to the bottom, back to the mud. And with Atum's permission, it'll grow into a flower, bringing light in the midst of darkness."

Memi stares back into the eyes of his friend, knowing such words are poetic, yet true.

---

[77]   James Henry Breasted. Ancient Records of Egypt; Part One, § 408

[78]   *Scribes who made false entries in the public books or deleted something from the register, as well as those who substituted documents, had both hands cut off.*

Diodorus Siculus, *Historic Library* Vol 1, Chap. 78,
after a translation by Julius Friedrich Wurm

"Corruption versus corruption equals corruption," Thut-nefer concludes harshly.

"Corruption. What corruption? How do you fight corruption in the heart? Stay pure. Think of the lotus, as it blooms in the morning light. Its beauty is as the horizon of heaven. A beacon of fire in the dark night.

Hold your course, helmsman, even though you must throw out the excess ballast to steady your bark."

Thut-nefer's gaze lazily takes in the six columns towering high above he and his friend. The roof, made of massive slabs of stone, is perfectly aligned and a sensual sight, pleasing to the eye.

More and more scribes begin to approach in search of the cool shade offered by these great columns. He nudges his friend's foot with his sceptre.

"Let's go, Memi" he orders curtly, dragging himself away from the architectural marvel.

*   *   *

Chapter 14

As Thut-nefer and Memi arrive at the old willow, Ibeby is in deep conversation with a few fishermen.

The sun is at its highest, reflecting on the water along the river bank, creating a distinct shimmering. Only the black mud refuses to budge, staying dark and sober.

The fishermen shove the reed and papyrus punt off the bank, then wait, for the few moments it takes before the current picks them up, to start rowing.

"Life, prosperity, health," the scribe calls out to the priest, standing by on the bank. He turns around to greet his newfound friend.

"I have some news for you! The fishermen know the whereabouts of your friend, Nar. He's in Khonsu,[79] waiting for his trading vessel to be loaded."

"That's good news," Thut-nefer answers, relieved to know his friend is well.

Ibeby's freshly shaven head turns pink, as he silently acknowledges Thut-nefer's gratitude.

"You know, Ibeby, our neighbor, the nobleman attacked and pilfered our bee colonies. There is now no honey for the

---

[79] Heracleopolis . . . modern day Beni Suef

feast, and everyone's upset. I thought that maybe your wisdom could enlighten me as to how I or we can approach this evil man and teach him a lesson that he will not readily forget. His greed is blinding him to the virtues of good neighbourliness that have been taught to us by the ancient scripts."

"The spell of the scorpion-goddess Serqet driveth back thy might. Stand still, stand still and retreat through her spell,[80]" Ibeby exclaims, vexed by what he hears from Thut-nefer.

"Greed is an illness of our times, and only a snake will protect you against that insatiate neighbor. I shall prepare a charm and spell for you to use against him. Death comes to the snake because of its love of biting.

But, I must warn you. Its chief matter is purity. If you do not apply purity to it, it will not succeed. Purity is eternal. So, stay pure, my friend, in order that you may succeed."

"Yes, priest of Serqet, you honour me with your knowledge," responds Thut-nefer.

"I shall follow your instructions. The measure is the eye of Re, its abomination is the one who takes. As for a grain measurer who multiplies and subtracts, his eye will seal up against him.[81]"

He takes a step closer towards the priest while watching him fiddle with the amulets dangling on his staff.

"So, in reality, the black earth is truly all we have—the land and our connection to it, and in between is Maat.

As long as we connect, respect, and honour the earth, then our hearts can be truly joyous and thus pure," Thut-nefer wraps up proudly.

Ibeby coughs and shakes his head. "When we use love to hoe the earth, the earth's energy can fill our soul with its

---

[80]   A. W. Budge, *Legends of the Gods*, 1912, pp.143
[81]   Teachings of Amenope

rhythms and reset us to be in balance with the universe," Ibeby adds impatiently, as if he's lecturing one of his disciples.

He thumps his heavy staff on the ground.

"Like our noble King Scorpion of ancient times, holding the hoe and leading his people."

"Mer[82]," Thut-nefer sighs after a moment of silence, letting the sound of the word roll down his tongue.

"Yes, dear Sesh," the priest agrees, now looking directly into Thut-nefer's hazel green eyes for the first time.

The scribe steadies his eyes, feeling slightly taken aback, a nervous tingle again spreading to his fingers, as when the lotus' fragrance appeals to his sensitivities.

The priest's unquivering gaze stands its ground, not flinching, he continues.

"The stronger the civilization, the more heightened the balance. Human actions must uphold Maat as the most important value in their lives. It cannot be left to the King only, and especially if he has failed to do his duty."

The priest pauses for a moment.

"Look deep in your heart, young Sesh, and you'll find these words only confirm what is already there.

Yes, its chief matter is purity of heart. It is the fulcrum of the balance, like Men-nefer being the fulcrum of the two lands.

Reed and papyrus are placed on the double-door of the House of Ptah. That means Horus and Seth, pacified and united.

They fraternize, so as to cease quarrelling in whatever place they might be, being united in the House of Ptah, the

---

[82]   Mer. The hieroglyphic sign is the hoe which means love.

'Balance of the Two Lands,[83]' in which the northlands and the southlands have been weighed."

Thut-nefer bends over and clasps a handful of black earth from close to the river bank, takes a deep breath of the mud, and looks up at the short, thin priest towering above him.

A pair of lanner falcons looks down curiously, perched high up on the branches of a nearby willow, stretching their wings in the gentle breeze.

The scribe stares at the two birds with amazement, watching their antics together.

"The truth that makes alive is the hardest thing to face," acknowledges Thut-nefer, "just like poison streaming through your blood canals, slowly but agonizingly, getting closer and closer to the heart, o' purified one."

"Does the smell of kemet, the black earth, invoke your sense of the love of creation and its creator, o' Sesh?" The priest replies quickly, not giving the scribe the chance to regain his composure.

Pointing his finger at the falcons, he recites a scriptural passage with great relish.

"Be vomited, o' poison, I adjure thee to come forth on the earth. Horus uttereth a spell over thee; Horus hacketh thee in pieces; he spitteth upon thee.

Thou shalt not rise up towards heaven, but shalt totter downwards, o' feeble one, without strength, cowardly, unable to fight, blind, without eyes, and with thine head turned upside down.

Lift not up thy face. Get thee back quickly, and find not the way. Lie down in despair, rejoice not, retreat speedily, and show not thy face, because of the speech of Horus, who is perfect in words of power.

---

[83]   M. Lichtheim: *Ancient Egyptian Literature*, Vol.1, pp.51-55

The poison rejoiced, but the hearts of many were very sad thereat. Horus hath smitten it with his magical spells, and he who was in sorrow is now in joy.[84]"

*   *   *

---

[84]   *A. W. Budge, Legends of the Gods, 1912, pp. 143ff*

Chapter 15

The Overseer of the Fields checks the boundary stone and beckons Thut-nefer to read the oath.

"I swear by the great god that is in heaven that the right boundary stone has been set up, and that I'll measure accordingly."

The sun rises silently above the horizon, giving off a crisp morning glow.

It is going to be a long day, Thut-nefer thinks to himself, as he begins to collect some ripe wheat husks to hand to the overseer, as samples of quality of this year's harvest.

The overseer of the fields simply grunts and packs them away in a linen pouch, careful not to blight his comfortable sitting position.

It is obvious that the burly man is not at ease out in the open; rather, he prefers to be sitting in the comfort of an administrative building, where all his needs are immediately taken care of by his underlings.

He grunts again in displeasure. Thut-nefer takes the cue, and nods to Memi to unwind the calibrated cord spun from palm fibre.

He adjusts the knots between each, measuring out one cubit[85] at a time, and hands the end to Thut-nefer, who plants his sceptre behind the boundary stone and ties the cord to it.

"Move out, Memi, northwards to the next stone," he instructs loudly, hoping to pacify the overseer, who begins to look like he is going to fall asleep.

Thut-nefer feels the tug of the cord, as it reaches its full length, and waits for Memi's signal to move out towards him.

By the time he reaches Memi, they both are out of audible range. They simultaneously sigh in relief, glad to be away from the authoritarian figure of the overseer.

"This man is even worse than the one we had at the cattle count," Memi remarks quietly. "Doesn't the King have any loyal administrators? It seems our good governor has bought them all.

Soon, we won't have a king, or at best, a king who is kept like the sacred animals in their pens at the temples," Memi comments softly, looking over in the direction of the overseer.

"Are you finally coming round to what I have been telling you?" Thut-nefer whispers back.

He then shouts, "Give me the readings, Memi!" while pulling out a scroll and retracting his reed pen from behind his ear and wig.

"Make sure you count the knots correctly," he mumbles, chewing on his reed pen, before he dips it into the palette and scribbles the preliminary figures on the scroll.

He digs his sceptre in the ground again and gives Memi the sign to move out once more.

The sun, now high on the horizon, turns the fields of ripe wheat into a golden sea. Thut-nefer marvels at the spectacle,

---

[85]   One cubit = 51 cm

setting aside all the discomforts he feels, listening to the rustle of the wheat in the gentle morning breeze.

Not far off, he spots a few wheat-eaters, small birds daintily perched just below the husks, pecking away at the ripe wheat, grain after grain, too busy to take any notice of him.

He thinks of shooing them off, but, at the last minute, refrains.

The governor and his henchmen grow fat at the expense of all other living beings, he considers. *Let them enjoy what they can, while they can.*

He scans the adjacent fields and spots a lone Nahet tree[86] standing high above the horizon of the sea of wheat, like the cedar mast of one of the King's ships returning from the Land of Punt.

Thut-nefer pauses for a moment, thinking of his master and mentor.

Brandish your ushabti and let it fly! O Khentiki, you taught us fair and well! With the Was sceptre in one hand and the ushabti in the other, we shall overcome. May Atum bless your heart!

He feels the cord going taut again. "Move out, Sheshu," he hears Memi's shout across the field, frightening off the wheat-eaters and his thoughts in a flutter.

The overseer had long gone to seek the shelter of his workplace and his petty comforts, leaving the two scribes to finish off the measurements.

Memi beckons Thut-nefer with the wave of his arm to approach, in order for him to take the last reading at the southernmost border stone. When he arrived to gather the measurement, the two men stood together at the point where they had started from.

---

[86]   Ficus sycomoros

Thut-nefer takes the last reading and scribbles the figures on his papyrus scroll. Sitting on the border stone, too tired to stand up any longer, oblivious to the outside world, he tries to sort out all the figures in a comprehensive order, while the numbers are still fresh in his mind.

The smoke of a fire brings him back to reality. He looks over at Memi, who sits cross-legged on the ground, taking some grilled wheat husks from the fire and rubbing them between his hands, then flicking the husks of wheat into the air, with the intention of separating the chaff from the seeds.

The seeds land in his lap, while the chaff floats up into the late afternoon breeze. He walks over to Thut-nefer and drops a handful of the roasted wheat into his lap, grinning from ear to ear.

The hunger pangs in Thut-nefer's stomach could no longer be disregarded.

"That's all we have left to eat. There are half a jug of beer and a little water to wash down your meal, O Scribe of the Holy City of Men-nefer," he states, laughing.

"One must be satisfied with what one has. That's the secret to happiness."

Thut-nefer pops the crunchy seeds into his mouth, and begins chewing slowly. The taste of the wood smoke is overpowering, yet delicious. He accepts the earthenware jug of beer gratefully and takes a couple of small sips.

"Good, good, Memi. You are a real master of procurement! If only the governor knew, he would whisk you off into his service, instead of allowing you to languish out in the fields, counting wheat husks!"

Memi's laughter rings out loudly, making the donkey snuff and stomp his hoof, ready to bray, shattering the surrounding tranquility.

* * *

Soon it would be dark. The two scribes hasten their pace in an effort to reach the local administrative building, before the sun disappears behind the horizon.

The day's figures had to be handed over to the overseer, who in turn would hand them over to the supervisor, to be compared to last year's numbers.

From all these figures, they would work out the probable yield, which then would be compared to the actual yield after the threshing was done.

The samples of the wheat grains in each district would be tested for their quality to give an overall picture of the year's harvest. Nothing would be left to chance, with hundreds of thousands of precise figures being minutely recorded by an army of scribes, each one contributing to the overall picture.

The two scribes walk in silence toward the overseer's office, each one immersed in his own thoughts, with each holding onto the donkey from the middle of its rigging, like young mothers dragging their unwilling toddlers.

"You two scribes, what's the hurry? Are you afraid of being tied to the stake?"

Thut-nefer hears the jeers of a group of scribes sitting around the edge of the well-worn pathway.

"Have you seen the overseer?" he retorts.

"You won't see the likes of him. He will be long gone, basking in comfort, waiting for your lot to show up," a scraggly young scribe replies, leaning against his donkey.

"Well, what are you all waiting for? It'll soon be dark," Memi asks.

"We're waiting for justice," comes the answer from one in the crowd, and then a burst of laughter.

The scraggly young scribe stands up straight and points his sceptre at the group.

"They are afraid of being the first ones to arrive."

"If you're waiting for justice, you will probably be waiting for a very long time," Thut-nefer answers, jabbing the donkey in the neck with his fingers, to get it to move along.

He hears the chorus of jeers ring in his ears, like a bunch of women wailers at a common burial . . . but decides to ignore it, for the sake of peace.

At last, the administrative building is in sight. The sun's golden rays light up the vast papyrus-shaped columns at the entrance.

As it dips down closer to the horizon, the rays penetrate deep inside the building, giving it a supernatural impression, like a heart thumping out streams of blood.

"Are you ready for this?" Thut-nefer inquires, casually hoping to hide his sense of apprehension.

Memi's face tightens at the question. Thut-nefer looks at his friend, the anxiety clearly apparent in his eyes. His feet are stuck to the ground, like broken dead reeds transfixed in the mud amidst a receding flood.

"Just stay behind me, and stay quiet. Tie up the donkey over there, near where the cowards are still sitting by the pathway," Thut-nefer mentions, quietly looking around for any other scribes.

Briefly gazing up at the sky, he recites a silent prayer, while fumbling for the frog amulet that Ibeby had given him. He eventually grasps it, and inconspicuously slides it under the linen belt of his kilt, next to his skin.

"We are the resurrection," he groans out loud, startling Memi. "Just think of the lotus bursting out from the swampy waters. From darkness to light, that is our solace. That is our strength. That is our resurrection."

He squeezes Memi's hand gently. "Let us face our burden; no man can escape his fate."

*   *   *

Thut-nefer and Memi stand quietly behind their supervisor of fields at the far end of the very large hall.

Three officials lie prostrate before the supervisor of supervisors, who, in turn, bows to the governor, with his right arm pressed to his heart.

"These officials have been caught falsifying their records," he declares, not daring to look up directly at the governor.

"Take them out and tie them up at the stake. Give them a good beating to remind them that the punishment for falsifying records and false entries in the public books is chopping both hands off."

The governor looks around him with an air of grandeur, fully aware that no one dares to oppose his decisions.

"And . . ." he pauses for a moment to maximize the effect of what he is about to say, ". . . to remind them that I have a big heart, a kind heart. No official of mine ever forgets that."

He lets a deep laugh rumble out from the depths of his protruding belly.

"I am the beginning and the end of mankind, since nobody like myself existed before, nor will he exist; nobody like me was ever born nor will he be born. I surpassed the feats of the ancestors, and coming generations will not be able to equal me in any of my feats within this million of years.[87]"

The governor is sitting on a large chair, intricately carved of the best woods imported from faraway lands. The smooth linen he wears is of the finest, reserved only for royalty.

---

[87]   The biography of Ankhtifi

Comfortably propped up by several pillows and nestled on the large wooden chair, he leans forward and taps his golden rings on the armrest. The sound of the tapping on the luxurious wood echoes through the large hall, causing the audience to hold its breath.

The governor gazes down from his elevated position with scorn. His dark piercing eyes survey the hall relentlessly, waiting for any opportunity to pounce on anyone committing the slightest error in protocol. He strokes his kilt tenderly, waiting.

In his right hand, he holds a chalice in the shape of a lotus blossom, emblazoned with lapis lazuli and turquoise. He raises it to his mouth and drinks, then hands it to his servant, who quietly replenishes it.

Finally, he waves his hand to the supervisor of supervisors to proceed. The "offending officials" are raised off the ground and escorted out by four burly men; no doubt, the governor's loyal henchmen.

Behind the governor, a servant is fanning an alabaster incense bowl, allowing the sweet smoke to engulf the large hall, giving off an ambiance of a banquet, rather than a proceeding.

The supervisor of fields approaches slowly, bows to the governor, as is customary, and hands his scrolls to the head scribe to be checked.

The two young scribes, still at the far end of the hall, wait impatiently, knowing full well that it is their work now under careful scrutiny. The silence is unbearable, and only the constant swoosh of the hand fan breaks the monotony.

The supervisor of supervisors finally lays their papyrus scroll on a pile next to the governor and thumps his heavy wooden staff on the ground in acknowledgement.

They had survived, even though their work had been minutely dissected by the best of scribes. No errors had been found, and they were finally waved off like common geese herders blocking the passage of a nobleman and his entourage.

A shroud of darkness engulfs Men-nefer, as Thut-nefer and Memi walk silently out of the administrative building.

An overwhelming sense of relief settles down on them, like the dust free clarity following a turbulent sandstorm. Thut-nefer looks at his friend compassionately.

The scribes they had met earlier now stand outside the main portal, waiting to be ushered in by the overseer of fields. Their faces convey an unmasked fear of authority.

Thut-nefer stares at them in delight. *Where is their laughter and jeering now, those cowards?* he thinks. Their sullen faces return his stare, hoping to catch a glimpse of his face in the dark.

"Two officials beaten at the stake . . . where is your justice now?" Thut-nefer barks at them, risking to be overheard by some passing magistrate.

Memi grabs him by the arm and pulls him away quickly, moving him towards the donkey, and then as far away from the building as he thinks will be safe. Only then does Memi let go of his arm.

"Comments like that will get us in deep trouble, Shesu. Come on, I'm exhausted! Let's go home."

A young boy warily approaches them carrying his worn out reed sandals in one hand and a pouch made of coarse linen in the other.

He pauses for a moment, before timidly addressing the two scribes.

"O' noble Sesh, are you Thut-nefer the scribe of our holiest of cities . . ."

"And who might you be, boy?" Memi asks suspiciously.

"I have a message and this pouch from Ibeby, Priest of Serqet. I've been waiting all afternoon for you. I was instructed to hand it over personally to Thut-nefer the scribe, o' Sesh," he mumbles in the local dialect of the markets.

The boy extends his filthy hands, offering the wriggling pouch.

"Be careful how you handle it, o' Sesh. It's a snake."

Thut-nefer hesitates for a fraction of a second, but quickly grabs the dirty linen bag with one hand. He feels the bag wiggle under his grip and almost drops it in panic.

"You can go now, boy, and thank the priest," he declares pleasantly, hiding his revulsion. Walking over to his donkey, he drops the bag in one of the baskets dangling from the beast's back.

Memi looks at his friend in amazement, unsure what to expect next.

"It's alright, Memi," he cajoles. "Drop your writing gear on top and let us be on our way!"

By the crossroad, Memi stumbles along on the uneven track and breaks the silence.

"It sure is a dark night."

"The moon will rise soon and I need the darkness to get rid of this snake," Thut-nefer comments mysteriously, his voice quivering slightly at the thought of what he is about to do.

Unable to see Memi's face in the dark, he coughs and explains softly to his silhouette.

"I've got to throw it over into the neighbour's garden. And what's worse, is that I have to get it out of the bag and over the wall!"

"What mischief are you up to now, Sheshu? I trust you won't get yourself caught!"

"Don't worry, I'll be fine. You take the donkey home and I'll send someone round to pick it up tomorrow. If I don't see you for some reason, then have a good Djed pillar festival."

Thut-nefer grabs the linen pouch with the snake and dangles it menacingly in front of Memi's face. Bursting into laughter, he affectionately squeezes his friend's shoulder. Without a word, he slips into the darkness, like a common thief.

The obscurity and silence of the opaque night intrigues Thut-nefer. *Is that a sign?* he wonders.

He looks over his shoulder warily, half expecting a lone night watchman to accost him. Not far away, Thut-nefer can just make out the neighbour's wall, which is built along a small canal.

Taking a moment to get his bearings, he looks for the lowest part in the fortification. He approaches cautiously and undoes the rough string tied to the sack, his stomach squirming.

He begins to climb up a section of the wall that had lost its mud plastering. Halfway up, Thut-nefer grabs hold of the snake just below the head and flings it over the wall.

Losing his foothold in the process, he comes crashing down, landing with a loud thud. Instinctively, he rolls over to his side, hoping to break his fall. By doing so, he inadvertently slides down the canal's steep embankment of slippery mud.

The dark, filthy brown water of the canal feels cold on his skin upon impact. Not far off, he hears the muffled voices of men approaching. Safeguarding his position, he lays down low among the floating debris and tall reeds growing along the waterway.

"Give me strength, o' lotus," he thinks to himself, as he holds his breath and lowers himself deeper into the fetid water, fearful of being discovered. The stench of the stagnant water repulses him.

How does purity exist among the rats and filth of this torpid water?

Thut-nefer can now hear the voices quite distinctly. Quietly, he camouflages his face with a fistful of mud.

"You men, look over there!" a brusque voice echoes through the night.

Recognizing it as that of the overseer of the nobleman's estate, he lowers himself a little deeper, until the dark putrid waters reach his nose. He senses a dozen water rats all around him, but he does not move. Thut-nefer closes his eyes in desperation, waiting for the men to pass.

Behind his closed eyelids the light is blinding. Rising from the dank waters in his mind's eye, he witnesses a sacred spectacle, a vision of a lotus flower opening its petals, revealing its bright yellow stamens to the darkness of the universe.

Not far off, a bullfrog's low, groaning croak calls out to the scribe. Basking in the dazzling light of his vision, Thut-nefer's body and mind grow numb, and he sinks within, immersed in a state of silent bliss. Fear no longer capturing his spirit, he allows himself to drift towards his fate.

The bullfrog croaks again.

"Try over there," snorts the overseer, panting heavily, directing his men efficiently.

Suddenly, a rush of cane comes crashing down between the reeds, so close that Thut-nefer feels the hiss just before it strikes the water's surface.

Maintaining his vigilant calm in the water, Thut-nefer continues to float within his own inner pool of light.

"Hit harder, you swine!" the overseer repeats, shoving one of his men out of the way. "Over there!"

The cane comes crashing down once more.

A fat waterfowl, nesting nearby, jumps over his head in panic, creating noisy squawks and a rumbling flutter in the quiet night. The men retreat slowly, seemingly satisfied that there is no one around, but water birds.

A shadow of darkness enshrouds Thut-nefer once again. Blinded by the brightness of his vision, the insignificance and obscurity of a mere mortal being no longer matters to him. He opens his mind's eye to see light alone, and he realizes the playing out of his fate is beyond his control.

It is time to stand up, now, and go where I'm drawn and be who I am, irregardless.

Thut-nefer crawls out of his dark slimy tomb and up onto the dry embankment. The cool evening breeze causes his body to tremble.

"Horus has fallen down because of his Eye," he affirms, reciting to himself to steady the quivering. "The bull has rolled down because of his testicles. Fall ! Roll down !⁸⁸"

Lifting himself up slowly, he begins to walk, only to notice his sandals are no longer on his feet. The black mud has sucked and swallowed them into perpetuity.

I will walk back barefoot, like the Kings of old, he consoles himself, picking up his pace.

Thut-nefer follows the narrow track along the small canal. Finding no one, he cuts across a field and pauses for a moment in the shelter of a palm grove, anticipating sunrise.

His body aches and the skin around his arm and legs are badly scratched by the razor sharp leaves of the reeds. He wishes for Ibeby's wisdom, like the early morning clarity beginning to engulf his vision. The previous night's escapade had taught him a vital lesson.

---

88   Pyramid text of Unas: **Utt. 277**
      418:

Rising with great brilliance, Ra shines on his domain, he cogitates, watching the sun come up gracefully between the palms.

How can I live the truth, when truth itself is obscured and hidden behind a complex wall of falsities?

I did everything Ibeby told me to do. I've kept a pure heart from the start, yet here I am, aching and bruised.

Are these just more of the subtle contradictions of life, not unlike a lotus rising from a decaying swamp?

Not looking back, Thut-nefer sprints across the last wheat field adjacent to home. He climbs the wall of his family residence with ease, knowing well where to place each foot.

It's been some time since I've used this route, he chuckles to himself, as he lowers his bruised body carefully down over the other side.

Making sure nobody has seen him, he ducks under the vine trellises and makes his way silently towards the house.

*   *   *

Chapter 16

After a wash and a short nap, Thut-nefer painfully moves to the window of his room and looks up at the morning sky.

"It's a beautiful day for the Djed pillar festival," he mumbles to himself.

He could see his mother already up and hustling about, giving instructions to the womenfolk. He dresses quickly and hurries down to see about his breakfast. On his way to the kitchen quarter, he stops by the lotus pond and sits down for a moment to soak in the tranquility.

The pond is a hive of activity—the red dragonflies swooshing back and forth; a kingfisher perched on a papyrus stalk, patiently looking down into the pond, waiting for a small fish to surface. Thut-nefer stares at the bird, finding himself drawn in by the bright turquoise feathers on its back.

Suddenly, it plunges headlong into the murky waters of the pond, disappearing for a brief instant, leaving behind the gently swaying papyrus stalk.

Resurfacing again with a small fish in its beak, it flies off, the bright turquoise feathers on its back reflecting the sun's rays, creating a flash of blue lightning streaking through the air.

Thut-nefer is amazed by the spectacle unfolding before him. *So much beauty in the truth that makes alive, and so much rot surrounding the beauty. Yet somehow, beauty exceeds it, giving us a lifeline to hold on to . . . hope.*

He recites an old curse, under his breath, letting it fly like the kingfisher moments before, while gently rubbing the cuts on his legs.

"Your deed be against you, what you will do will be against you, o zkzk-serpent . . ."[89]

Thut-nefer sits down to breakfast in his usual spot, next to the oven. The low, wooden table had already been prepared. Meryt-ra, the mistress of the house, looks superb in her outfit to celebrate the Djed pillar festival. Her eyes are freshly made up with black kohl, and her linen dress is impeccable.

"Good morning, my son. What happened to you?" she asks scornfully, yet with concern, as she sees her son's injured legs.

"I slipped and fell," he answers, meekly diverting his eyes towards the food.

Meryt-mi-hapi hands him some hot fresh loaves, just out of the oven. Thut-nefer takes them, gratefully hoping to change the subject.

"I have news of your brother, o' Beloved of the Nile. He is well and on his way back!"

Meryt-mi-hapi's eyes lighten up with pleasure at the good news, as she watches him eat.

"Go and fetch some fresh milk for the master," Meryt-ra orders.

Thut-nefer looks at the girl, as she walks away, her firm buttocks swaying through the tight linen dress the mistress had given her for the occasion of the festival.

"Your uncle has sent a courier for the land papers," Meryt-ra intervenes, unable to hold back her displeasure.

---

[89] Utt. 276. 417. Unas Pyramid Text

"I told him you weren't in. I think the governor is getting impatient."

"I have hidden them. Please, Mother, this is strictly between you and me. He has no right to confiscate my lands. I have been taught to follow the ancient scripts, and so I shall, come what may."

"I fear for you, my son. This governor is notorious for getting his way."

"Fear not, mother, o' beloved of Ra. All injustice must have an end. It is a matter of patience and endurance. So it is written in the scriptures of old."

*   *   *

"Master, Master," the young houseboy calls out. He walks up to Thut-nefer, holding a pair of new sandals in both hands, gleaming from ear to ear.

His coarse linen kilt is clean and well kept befitting the occasion. Thut-nefer had finished dressing in his finest kilt and was just slipping the frog amulet into its place.

"The master sandal maker has sent you these. He hopes they are agreeable to you," he stutters, the scar on his chin still not wholly healed.

Thut-nefer looks at the boy with affection.

"You will make a good sandal-bearer, boy. Quiet and faithful. Nobody asks of you to carry such a burden, rather it will be thrust upon you. Who knows, maybe you will understand one day."

He tries on the new sandals and takes a few steps towards the doorway of the house.

"Good, good. Couldn't be better. Come on, sandal-bearer! You're going to watch the running of the bulls around the white walls[90] with me today!"

Thut-nefer looks at his household proudly, all in their best dress, a sight that pleases his eye.

"Are we ready to go?" Thut-nefer asks, bemused, watching their unconcealed enthusiam leap out of their eyes.

"I will lead the first group and Shendwa the second."

The women break into a spontaneous and happy ululation, drowning him out.

Thut-nefer decides to get a move on and steps through the outer portal first, followed by the mistress and Meryt-mi-hapi, expertly balancing a reed mat on her head. The boy brings up the rear, his faithful sling tied around his waist.

As they near the major thorough-fare, the sheer excitement of the mock battle between good and evil electrifies the crowds assembled around the white walls of this ancient city. Groups of people, friends and families all nestled together, watch the spectacle with great enthusiasm.

"The Djed pillar has been raised and the people are paying homage to their symbol of eternity," Thut-nefer shouts uncontrollably above the people's chants, trying to capture his mother's attention.

Meryt-mi-hapi lays out the new reed mat on the ground for the mistress to sit on, waving away a young hawker peddling some dried figs.

"And soon they'll be driving the bulls around the city to honour the founding of our eternal capital!" he continues unabashed, shouting to no one in particular, clearly the enthusiasm taking a hold of him.

---

90 City of Men-nefer (Memphis)

"Look, look, master!" the boy calls out excitedly, pointing toward the approaching bulls.

"Indeed! What a majestic sight!" Meryt-ra adds cheerfully, thrilled by the spectacle.

The first wave of bulls passes by. Shouting and coaxing their animals, in the hope of keeping their formation tight, the herdsmen drive on relentlessly.

The ecstatic and unified chant of the spectators drowns out the shrill commands of the head herdsman as he passes by, brandishing his heavy wooden staff, as if it were merely a twig.

Thut-nefer notices it's the same old herdsman who he had met at the old sycamore. Their eyes meet momentarily. The old herdsman waves his staff in a salute, his eyes shining through the dust.

Thut-nefer raises his Was sceptre, and graciously acknowledges the salute, incredulously watching this man be in command of his men *and* the animals so well.

Feeling the warm touch of Meryt-mi-hapi next to him, he turns around, only to see his mother beckoning him from a short distance, signalling to him she has had enough and wishes to return home.

He grabs Meryt-mi-hapi's arm inconspicuously and gives her a tight squeeze. She responds by gently brushing against him. Thut-nefer feels the fire igniting in his heart and body.

The din of the crowd around him fades away, and he only hears the pounding of his heart, like the beat of the lotus waking up from its winter sleep, unrolling its first leaves in anticipation for the first euphoric blossom of the season.

"Tomorrow, comes the more lofty of the two feathers[91] and King Ibi's procession for the symbolic cutting of the first sheaths

---

[91]   Min: god of fertility

of wheat." Thut-nefer vaguely hears the man standing next to him, speaking to his son, over the throbbing of his heart.

The second wave of oxen passes by, their hooves pounding the ground like thunder. The crowd rises to view the pageantry, their collective consciousness becoming one pulsing sense of elation.

Ironically, Thut-nefer thinks, *this event is the very heart of this holiest of cities . . . yet the entire society is slowly sliding into decline.*

He pauses and looks out at the masses of onlookers. After a few moments, he sighs, and his reflections continue, his inner tone becoming increasingly sombre.

The dust settles. The flies return. The belly of the children rumble with the pangs of hunger, which can no longer be ignored.

Corruption holds fast, like a mongoose burying its sharp teeth into its slithering prey, unable to let go, even if it wants to, for fear of being bitten. Another poor harvest. More hunger. Maat is in disorder.

The crowd roars in unison again, as the third wave of bulls passes by.

Having spotted Thut-nefer, Memi fights his way through the crowd towards his friend.

"The mistress Meryt-ra is tired. We must go. Come by later," Thut-nefer shouts to his friend, unable to reach him.

Memi acknowledges by raising his sceptre and is instantaneously sucked back into the multitude, vanishing amongst the sea of excited faces.

Thut-nefer takes hold of his mother, while also looking around for the boy. Meryt-mi-hapi grabs him by the scruff of the neck, desperately trying to balance the reed mat on her head.

Closing ranks, they push their way through the dense crowd and head for home.

*   *   *

Thut-nefer stares deep into the lotus pond, his bruised face reflecting in the calm, afternoon waters.

He is happy to be back home, away from the maddening crowds, now able to enjoy the tranquillity and safety of his garden.

Below his image, a catfish suddenly breaks the surface, while chasing smaller fishes, perturbing his reflection. Thut-nefer's sullen look mirrors the wretched feeling inside of him. He moves his aching body into a more comfortable position.

Memi, who has just arrived, is worried by his friend's fatigued looks. He passes him an earthenware jug. Barely aware, Thut-nefer takes a swig of the half hin of beer and gently eases the jug to the ground next to him.

"It's a good time for you to disappear now, during the rush of the crowds, and while the governor is busy filling up his coffers from the sweat of the poor wretches working the land," Memi whispers to his friend.

"I'll try to cover for you as best as I can in the coming days," he rattles on nervously, trying to reassure himself, as well as his friend.

"You're a good man and a dear friend," Thut-nefer replies, trying to hold back his emotions . . . to no avail, a tear forming in the corner of his eye.

"Those thugs worked you over well, by the looks of things."

"They cornered me when I was alone, out in the fields. Once I got back from the festival, I thought I would go out for a walk. They said that this was just a warning and if I didn't hand over the deed to the governor voluntarily, things would get a lot worse."

Memi looks at Thut-nefer compassionately, inspecting and scrutinizing his friend's face, which bears the cuts and bruises of his violent encounter.

"The hissing of the snake is more effective than the braying of the donkey[92]," Memi explodes, unable to hold back his anger any longer.

Memi stops to, observe the frustration cloud up Thut-nefer's face, like an approaching storm devastating the sun's brightness to an opaque red.

Continuing, he adds, "I heard from my father that the governor has ordered his thugs to confiscate your plot of land, with or without the title. And, I came here to warn you."

He falls silent again.

"The snake on which one steps ejects a strong poison[93]," Thut-nefer counters harshly, his eyes turning to his friend fiercely.

Then, softening his stance again almost immediately, he pats Memi on the shoulder.

"Thanks, dear friend, for the warning. I think I'll do as you advise and disappear for a while, first thing in the morning. So, if you'll excuse me, I'm going to try and get some rest. May you live in peace, health and prosperity!"

*   *   *

The thin line of light in the horizon is proclaiming another glorious day. With the last eerie forlorn cry of the Thicknee, as it wishes to bid its farewell to the comfort of the night, Thut-nefer approaches the stables quietly to fetch his donkey.

---

[92]   M. Lichtheim, *Ancient Egyptian Literature*, Vol 3, p.170ff
[93]   Ibid

The morning air is crisp, causing him to briefly shiver. The donkey, not accustomed to be saddled up in the dark, lets out a loud snort, causing the boy to awaken. He looks at his master wide-eyed.

"Quiet boy," Thut-nefer whispers, "help me with the rigging."

The boy jumps up to his feet and quickly obeys.

Thut-nefer could still hear his mother's voice ringing in his ears, pleading with him not to go, until her eyes were red with painful tears, the black kohl streaking across her face giving her that fearful look.

That was one of the few moments he had seen his mother really lose her composure.

Leaving the comfort of his home for the unknown, Thut-nefer decides to take the plunge into the deep dark abyss opening up in his heart. The uncertainty of how things would play themselves out disturbed him the most.

But, one thing he knew for certain, was that he would not break his Maat. Dead set against all forms of corruption, no matter where they were prevalent, he would defiantly stand his ground, at all costs.

The blessings of all the knowledge that has been passed down to me by teachers and mentors, he declares to himself, *like the roots of the lotus anchored in the depth of the swamp, resisting the currents, give me hope and strength against my own apprehensions.*

He leads the donkey out through the old wooden portal, trying not to gaze back. Out of the corner of his eye, he sees the houseboy standing not far from him.

"Go home, boy," he orders calmly, "and make sure you feed the dog well."

He turns around and watches the boy retreat reluctantly. Behind him, he catches a glimpse of a woman's figure wrapped in a coarse linen sheet, neatly balancing a wicker basket on her head.

Thut-nefer makes nothing of it and within moments, he disappears down the path leading away from the house.

It must have been hours before Thut-nefer thought it was safe enough to stop for a rest. His new sandals were aching his feet.

Once out of the white walls, he had kept away from major thoroughfares, not wanting to attract attention. A lone scribe wandering around on a festival day would seem suspicious.

Sitting down in the shade of a cluster of palm trees, Thut-nefer allows his donkey to graze on the wild grasses growing along the side of the dusty path.

In the distance, through the lifting fog he could just make out his mud hut. Thut-nefer dares not approach any closer, for fear of being spotted.

A group of men shuffling around, are busy preparing their morning meal, oblivious to their surroundings.

He takes a drink and the cool water refreshes him, as it gurgles out of the earthenware jug. Once finished, he stuffs the palm bark back into the top and prepares, once again, to move forward.

"O' Sesh," he hears someone whispering from behind a palm tree, startling him.

Instinctively, he grabs his sceptre, waiting for the figure to appear.

Meryt-mi-hapi approaches boldly, still balancing the wicker basket on her head. She looks at him meekly, with her big black eyes shining through the black kohl.

For a moment, he returns the gaze with extreme amazement, his eyes glued to the figure wrapped in a clean linen sheet.

"What are you doing here, girl?" he asks harshly, not wanting to appear too soft in front of her.

Deep down, though, he feels a sense of relief. A lotus bud is dangling around her neck, an informal pendant tied in the fashion of the local river people.

Somehow, Thut-nefer recognizes, the sense of evil foreboding seems to vanish in her presence. He fumbles for his Ptah amulet and strokes it for reassurance.

"I followed you, o' Sesh. Your destiny is mine."

Thut-nefer decides to move on. Memi's warning had turned out to be true.

The governor had not wasted any time, even if he was busy filling up his coffers with his brutal policy of taxation. He had usurped his land and broken his Maat.

There is no limit to greed, Thut-nefer ponders. *It sucks at you like an ailment of rot, poisoning the bloodstream, causing an imbalance of the body and mind, just like the Mighty River being poisoned by human greed causes the flood to be feeble.*

Hapi [94] *no longer flows with righteousness, and this, to the detriment of all living things. May we sing a hymn to the flood!*

*   *   *

---

[94]   The Nile

Chapter 17

Thut-nefer stands forlorn in a state of imbalance on the very day that people across the land celebrate the harvest of the grains. The festival of Min is their fertility festival, insuring continued life for the coming year.

He watches as a procession sets out from the temple. The King, followed by a white bull, believed to be sacred to Min, and a priest burning incense, walk steadily towards the fields that are to be harvested.

Carried high on a platform and draped in the finest of cloths by his proud carriers, a statue of Min, the god of fertility, looks over field upon field of ripe golden grains glittering in the sunlight.

Bringing up the rear, a lone priest carries bundles of holy lettuce grown at his temple.

Thut-nefer looks at the wheat swaying gently around him. The sight is pleasing to his eyes, and momentarily plugs the gaping hole in his heart. It is only a fleeting illusion flashing by, however; like the kingfisher retrieving its catch and leaving behind a streak of bright turquoise.

He could tell that it was going to be a bad harvest, once again, this year. The signs were plain for him, and all, to see.

"There is a fisherman's encampment not far from here," Meryt-mi-hapi stutters, venturing out to break the silence. She is not used to seeing Thut-nefer so quiet and sombre.

"We could find shelter there, if you so wish," she adds gently, not wishing to break his train of thought.

Thut-nefer feels remorse and walks around aimlessly in a lopsided circle. He tugs at his donkey to stop, knowing he must pull himself together.

Looking out ahead in front of them, he sees a small encampment of several mud huts next to a large canal. The huts are draped with nets and baskets hung out to dry.

The smoke of a fire is drifting towards them, bringing with it a succulent tang of grilled fish. Two simple reed boats are tied up along the banks of the canal, half hidden by the papyrus thickets.

A few young children sit with their feet in the water, gutting fish by the bank. They playfully splash each other. Thut-nefer hears the shrill shout of a woman ordering the children to stop playing and to get on with their task.

Thut-nefer recoils at the sights and smells, as he approaches the mud huts. The filth and squalor is unbearable to him.

He hesitates briefly, not knowing whether he should move on or turn back. Meryt-mi-hapi feels his hesitation and pulls at his arm.

"Yes, we may be poor and downtrodden, but we have our pride," she exclaims, looking at him directly without flinching.

"We live among the water, among hippos and crocodiles, yet our pride in life is our strength. We are shooed away, because of the stench of our fish and looked down upon, because we are of the lowliest of castes. Only the swine-herders are lower than us. Yet we risk our lives daily to feed hungry mouths. We are the true children of Osiris[95]."

---

[95] Osiris represents the element of water

He sees the shape of a crude knife dangling under her dress, an undetectable slit near the bulge, where undoubtedly she could reach for it quickly.

Her agility is clearly portrayed in her slim, yet sinewy figure. She stands up straight, still balancing the basket on her head. Fatigue seems not to bother her. A mischievous smile appears on her lips. She is on home territory, now, taking to it like a catfish slithering on the muddy bank, before dropping into the deeper brown waters.

The incredible shine in her black eyes brings Thut-nefer back to life, restoring his vigour. He bends over and picks up a handful of the black mud and raises his hand to his nose, inhaling deeply. "Geb[96]," he proclaims aloud.

"Pride in life is our strength," she prods, urging him to move on. Thut-nefer looks at Meryt-mi-hapi quizzically.

This girl never ceases to amaze me, he quietly reflects.

"Lead the way, o' beloved of the Nile," he commands with a smile.

Thut-nefer watches the children gut the fish, their faces and hands covered in dried fish blood and scales. Their agile hands slip into the belly of the fish, pulling out its intestines and bladder in one easy motion.

He leans against his donkey and takes in the landscape. *The poverty of these people is evident,* he surmises. *The governor is not leaving any stones unturned. No one can escape from his taxation policy and these poor people carry the brunt of it.*

Though his heart is troubled by what he sees, the breeze coming off the canal is cool and soothing to Thut-nefer's thoughts, like a balm of herbs applied to an open and infected wound.

"Shu," he gratefully sighs.[97]

---

[96]   Geb represents the earth.

[97]   Shu represents the air.

He hears the children giggling again.

They laugh, Thut-nefer observes, *even as the flies descend on them, like hoards of beggars brandishing their filthy food bowls for a bite to eat.*

Hunger and sleepless nights walk hand-in-hand, only to reawaken to the remembrance of Ra[98].

"O Atum, Lord of Totality!" He calls out, stretching his arms up high above his head towards the sky.

"Have mercy on us! You are the ultimate, unalterable state of perfection, like when the sun darkens in the day. Yes, totality, whereby the point where all elements join together at a given moment.

Only with mer[99] can one progress, holding unto one's balance, between the mountain of light and the mountain of darkness." Thut-nefer murmurs softly, confronting himself with his mirror image in the water.

He strokes the ear of his donkey affectionately, and then slaps him on the neck. The donkey snorts.

"This be so, until the day you submerge the world and plunge your living creatures in the dark waters of Nun.[100] And you will survive in the form of a serpent."

He coughs at the thought and takes a sip of cool water from his earthenware jug.

Again raising his arms above his head he continues,

"To say: The door of heaven is open, the door of earth is open, apertures of the heavenly windows are open, the steps of Nun are open, the steps of light are revealed by that one who endures always.

---

[98]   Ra represents the element of fire

[99]   Love

[100]   Nun: primeval waters

I say this to myself when I ascend to heaven, that I may anoint myself with the best ointment and clothe myself with the best linen, and seat myself upon the throne of Truth which makes alive.[101]"

Thut-nefer stands tall, holding his mind to a fervent thought of hope, banishing all the negativity that had so burdened him moments before.

No one can escape the truth which makes alive! Neither the governor nor the King, all will be plunged into the dark waters. Only those with pure hearts can follow the light to peace like the lotus engulfed in muddy waters mingling its light with that of Ra on the horizon. Fire and water.

Abiding one's time like the calendar—keepers waiting to sight the first rising of Sopdet[102] from their temples, excited to proclaim the New Year and the approaching flood. Truth which makes alive! That is our throne.

Nearby, Thut-nefer notices a Christ's thorn[103] tree standing proudly by the banks of the canal. He pulls at the donkey and gently strolls over to its beckoning shade.

Removing his sandals, he places his tired and blistered feet in the cool water. The thirsty donkey lowers its neck and eagerly sucks in the water.

Thut-nefer collects a few of the small, round fruit of the tree lying on the ground and nibbles at them contentedly, waiting for Meryt-mi-hapi to join him.

The sweetness of the small berries relaxes him. A sense of peace engulfs him, and all his worries seem to fade away, as if they belonged to another world.

---

[101] Pyramid text: utterance 503. Translation by Mercer.

[102] Helical rising of Sirius. Greek:Sothis

[103] Zizphus spina christi

Caught by Aker[104], the two lions seated back to back, one facing to the east and the other to the west, where night turns to day and day turns into night, Thut-nefer stares up at the horizon.

Yesterday and tomorrow meander by him, leaving him oblivious to the thoughts that had, moments earlier, preoccupied him. Now, their strain upon his heart and mind are not affecting him in the least, evaporating like the morning fog following sunrise.

"I have done Maat," he quietly asserts.

*   *   *

The cry of the Thicknee shatters the afternoon calm, like the cry of the Benu bird announcing that existence is coming into being. The silence of the primeval night is broken, and light and life is brought to creation.

"Oh there you are," Meryt-mi-hapi calls out cheerfully. "We've been offered shelter. I've arranged everything."

"It's so peaceful here," Thut-nefer answers gently, gazing at Meryt-mi-hapi and only now noticing how short she is.

Her aura is so much larger than her physical height and that's why I always mistook her for being that much taller, he muses, chuckling to himself in delight.

"Leave your donkey here and come and meet our host," she calls out with a big smile plastered across her face, enticing Thut-nefer with her dark shiny eyes.

Thut-nefer unties a piece of palm-fibre rope from around the donkey's neck and hobbles up its front legs.

---

104   Aker: They are also called 'Yesterday' and 'Tomorrow', as one lion faces towards the east where the sun rises and begins the new day, the other lion faces west where the sun sets and descends into the Underworld

They both move towards the encampment, evading the long lines of drying fishing nets dangling on wooden poles. A stone's throw away from where he had left his donkey and nestled between two rows of vine trellises, stands a dilapidated old mud hut.

"Welcome to our humble abode, o' holy scribe." The young fisherwoman proclaims as she steps out through the narrow doorway of her mud hut.

"Greetings, fisherwoman! Life, health and prosperity," Thut-nefer answers politely thumping his Was sceptre on the ground.

The fisherwoman spreads an old woven mat of reeds riddled with burn marks on the earth beneath a vine trellis in the shade. She beckons to Thut-nefer to come and sit down.

"Please accept a small meal of grilled fish, onions and dried bread."

Her tough and wrinkled face finally allows a smile to come forth. The black shadows under her eyes, Thut-nefer notices, are not kohl but the proof of a life of hard existence.

Thut-nefer's face registers an immediate compassion for this woman. He humbly acknowledges, *She is willing to share what meagre provisions she has for the sake of hospitality.*

He wanted to decline, but one stern look from Meryt-mi-hapi balancing the mud tray on her head, helps him decide to keep quiet, not wanting to offend either of them.

"Where are your men folk?" Thut-nefer inquires, finishing his meal. Mery-mi-hapi begins pouring some water from an old stained jug for him to rinse his hands.

"They're helping with the harvest. I'm salting the fish before it spoils," she answers in her fisher-people's drawl.

Thut-nefer leans forward slightly, trying to catch what she says. The pungent smell of the salted fish irritates his nostrils, even here out in the open.

"Are you a tax collector, o' Sesh?" she asks with a jitter in her voice. "You have very kind eyes, and you have no thugs with sticks."

"No, woman, I'm not. I'm here for my Maat," Thut-nefer answers promptly. He could see a sense of relief streak across her deeply sun-tanned face.

"Then you are welcome here among us."

*   *   *

Meryt-mi-hapi throws the linen fishing lines into one of the reed boats, along with a basket and a crude wooden harpoon. She holds onto the bow while Thut-nefer clambers on, and with one strong shove, the boat slithers off the muddy bank, like a crocodile slipping into the river.

The late afternoon sun shimmers along the surface of the water, causing an intense and blinding glimmer. The reed and papyrus boat glides softly through, just like the King's bark sailing through the sky in search of the Land of Reeds.[105]

Meryt-mi-hapi expertly nestles the boat quietly among some reeds and papyrus thickets without causing any ripples on the surface. She unwinds the fishing line and baits the hook with a small piece of date.

Carefully, she attaches a piece of broken pottery onto the line as a weight, and lowers it gently into the water. She winds her finger around the line and looks up at Thut-nefer, motioning to him to get the second line into the water.

He obeys and watches her wriggle the line slowly; the concentration on her face is intense. Moments later, he feels something nibbling at the end of the line.

---

[105]   Paradise

With a quick jerk, he pulls at his line, feeling the strong resistance of a hooked fish. Excitedly, he fights the struggling fish, pulling hand-over-hand, eventually landing it into the boat.

Meryt-mi-hapi quickly passes him the basket and, with one quick motion, he throws the fish into it.

"Very unusual, o' Sesh! You've caught an elephant trunk fish[106]!" she calls out hoarsely, breaking into a broad smile, her white teeth gleaming in contrast to her shiny, tanned face.

"They usually don't come this far into the canals. They prefer the deeper waters of the river. You know, this fish has an odd habit of swimming backwards," Meryt-mi-hapi explains jovially, poking it carefully with her forefinger.

"I know this fish, Meryt-mi-hapi," he answers. "My brother is a priest and he told me about it. It's the one that swallowed Osiris' phallus!"

"It's a sign, o' Sesh. Be careful on how you tread," she whispers mysteriously.

"Get back to fishing," he orders, trying to shake off the eerie cold feeling creeping up and down his spine.

"One of them once stung my brother, causing all his hairs on his body to stand on end[107]. It has strong magic."

She falls silent preferring not to continue. Thut-nefer baits his hook with a small piece of date and drops it back into the water.

He gropes for his frog amulet, to make sure it is still there, afraid that it might have fallen out of place.

---

[106] Mormyrus oxyrhychus (Kannume)

[107] A well grown specimen can give quite an electrical shock. From: 'Freshwater Fishes of Egypt'
Publication of National Biodiversity Unit. No. 9, 1997

Being so close to the water, Thut-nefer feels the importance of the frog; just knowing it is there has given him a tremendous boost in self-confidence.

He breathes in deeply, taking in the combination of scents all around him. He deliberates, *Ah, still, the odour of this muddy brown river water eventually overpowers them all.*

The presence of a strange tone overtakes Thut-nefer's settled consciousness. The surroundings he finds himself in look the same as always, peaceful and quiet, except for the occasional chattering of the waterfowl. *Yet,* he observes, *something is different.*

Meryt-mi-hapi reaches for the wooden harpoon, slowly and cautiously laying her hand on Thut-nefer's knee, squeezing it gently. He looks around, feeling a sense of danger.

"Lord of Stretches of Water and of Fishes," she whispers quietly, pointing in the direction of a papyrus thicket.

"Is that you, o' Sobek?" Thut-nefer stutters, stumbling over his own words as he desperately searches in the direction of where Meryt-mi-hapi had been pointing.

The paypyrus thickets are dense and bushy thus hindering his vision. Thut-nefer sees nothing.

Confused at first by the glare, he squints and focuses intensely on that one spot. The thickets begin to judder as the burly crocodile, completely camouflaged by a carpet of river algae, brushes against them.

Thut-nefer can now clearly see the trail through the algae, left behind by the great beast, while slowly making its way towards them.

*   *   *

"I felt your coming, o Sobek! So, we finally meet face-to-face. Are you here as my protector and will you avenge the wrongdoers who have caused me great anguish? O' Lord of Bakhu, dweller of the mountain of horizon, use Atum's wisdom and show me how to proceed."

The crocodile closes in slowly, its beady green eyes peering above the muddy brown waters, its nostrils taking in the scent of excitement dominating the air.

"Give him an offering, o' Sesh, quickly," Meryt-mi-hapi whispers urgently thrusting her flint blade into the stomach of the elephant nose fish, causing its intestines to dribble out.

"Throw him your fish!"

The moment the fish hits the water, the crocodile lunges for its prey, opening its mouth wide and snapping it shut in one quick motion. Keeping his eyes on the boat's occupants, he slowly disappears below the surface of the water.

Meryt-mi-hapi begins to move the boat out of the reeds and heads towards the encampment. She adjusts herself in the boat, turning to face the scribe.

"Lord of Stretches of Water and Fishes is pleased. We have given him his fish and left him his stretch of water. We will be safe, now."

"Lord of Bakhu lives in the mountain of horizon, where it is said that he has a palace made of pure carnelian," he comments, relieved to be out in the open away from the reeds and papyrus thickets.

Meryt-mi-hapi looks at Thut-nefer wide-eyed, with an incredulous look on her innocent face. He smiles back.

"Yes, pure carnelian," he repeats, slowly twitching his nose. "Like your eyes when they're on fire," he adds teasingly.

"Get your line back in the water, otherwise there won't be an evening meal," she utters coldly, her eyes now really on fire.

The glare of the sun on the water is slowly weakening, turning into a soft reflection of a lighter shade of orange.

Suddenly, Meryt-mi-hapi expertly pulls at her line, and begins landing a large catfish.

As it comes alongside the boat, she tightly grabs the black fish from behind the head with both hands. The catfish struggles with all its might, lashing out with its powerful tail. Thut-nefer slowly moves the basket closer to her, in an effort to stabilize the boat's equilibrium.

She thrusts the catfish into the basket, holding it down with one hand and reaching for her flint knife with the other.

With the precision of a surgeon, she slides the knife across its neck from just below the head, causing a gush of dark red blood to ooze out.

Satisfied that the fish no longer has the stamina to jump out of the basket, she looks proudly at Thut-nefer.

"Our dinner," she announces simply, washing the fish's dark blood off her hands in the brown murky waters of the canal.

"Yes, with Sobek's permission, we will have a feast; and with Atum's blessings, shall we eat," Thut-nefer remarks happily.

It had never occurred to him, before now, how simple life could be, when one is tuned into the larger dimension of nature, allowing it to take its course, for the better or for the worse.

That is the weight of the feather in the scale, he muses to himself.

"One values a scribe for his understanding, for understanding transforms an eager person[108]," Thut-nefer recites, remembering Khentiki's wise words and how he had drummed them into his memory. Only now did they make sense.

Meryt-mi-hapi nudges him and offers him a half hin jug of beer.

---

[108]   Dua Khety

"Thanks to your mother. She loves you. She gave me a basket full of provisions and made me swear by Ptah that I would feed you well."

Thut-nefer takes a long deep drink from the earthenware jug, allowing the thick, frothy liquid to settle in his stomach, before wiping away the telltale signs from his mouth.

He hands the jug to Meryt-mi-hapi, signaling her to drink. She takes it from him, hesitating momentarily, before raising it to her lips.

"We have a saying here among the folk, that if you drink after a man, you'll run after him," she sighs coyly, her eyes shining in the evening glow.

Thut-nefer raises his eyebrows in a comic fashion, watching her silhouette dance with the setting sun. She smiles at him.

"Is that fisherwomen tales?" he asks, lightly smiling back.

"No, not at all. That's wisdom from the ancients," she giggles, covering up her mouth with her hand.

She looks soberly at Thut-nefer, as she banks the reed boat just below the encampment.

The blackness of the night covers the earth, with Nut's nightly shroud only allowing the first stars to twinkle through.

"There's this large insect," she ventures shyly, as she collects the linen fishing lines and arranges them neatly, ready to be used again on the next outing.

"It's the size of your small finger. It lays its eggs in a blue lotus blossom, and then wraps its long, thin legs around the flower, not allowing it to open. The blossom struggles to open, but the strength of its body and legs keeps it shut."

Thut-nefer looks at Meryt-mi-hapi curiously, waiting for her to continue, watching her secure the reed boat. He collects the basket with the fish and hands it to her.

"Eventually the insect dies, and even in death, it embraces the flower, keeping it shut, protecting its eggs within."

She removes the fish from the basket and begins to cut open its belly. The fish beats its tail violently against the muddy ground in a final valiant effort to hold on to life.

"The embrace of death. And with death comes life," Thut-nefer comments, observing the sky, now filling up with stars.

He spots the three stars of Orion's belt, appearing from the eastern horizon.

"And what separates life from death, or death from life? Nothing, but the fine feather of one's Maat."

She tosses the guts into the canal.

"The catfish is a scavenger and not particularly clean. It'll eat almost anything, even the guts of its own kind. I prefer the tilapia, a clean fish. It's a vegetarian and its favourite food is the roots of the lotus," she counters, smiling mischievously.

"Come, o' Sesh, allow me to prepare the evening meal for you. I have a little bird's grease, and we can fry up the catfish and eat it with bread and beer."

Thut-nefer tosses her a small linen pouch with the festival spices. She catches it in the darkness, like a cat deftly snatching a river rat.

"Once you're done with the spice, please give it to the fisherwoman as a token of our appreciation."

Meryt-mi-hapi smiles, applauding Thut-nefer's kind gesture. Raising it to her nose, she breathes in the delicious aroma.

"Prepare the meal and add a little magic to it, girl. Let us look through Nature's eyes to reach Atum's blessings. Just as the nets of the fishermen catch fish, the scribe and his tools, catch live words and thoughts on papyrus.

It's very simple. What concerns turquoise? It is connected to Osiris' teeth. And what concerns gold? It's connected to the body of Ra, just as silver is connected to his bones and malachite to his eye. So be it."

Chapter 18

Thut-nefer unravels his travel mat, made from palm tree leaves, next to the warm embers of the fire and spreads out his linen blanket, like Nut spreading out her blanket of stars across the universe.

He had undone the donkey's rig for the night and had hobbled its front legs, not wanting it to stray too far away.

The night is alive with sound, as countless bullfrogs are busy out-croaking each other, in the hope of finding a long lost mate.

Thut-nefer settles down on his mat, letting the weight of the day disperse into the darkness of the night. His eyes wander over to Mery-mi-hapi, who is down by the canal washing up all the utensils.

For a poor, illiterate fisherman's daughter, she has a great mind on her shoulders, he reflects. *She can weigh out all her thoughts and actions precisely, knowing what to do and what not to do, whenever it is called upon her to do so.*

"Life is always the best school," he whispers aloud into the night.

Thut-nefer's mind wanders back to the banquet and the nobleman's daughter. She was very refined, educated and beautiful.

A father's girl pampered to the limits of wealth, yet somehow he couldn't see himself happy with a woman like that.

Meryt-mi-hapi walks up, balancing the mud tray and utensils on her head. Slowly, she lowers them gently to the ground, her body tense under the load.

Her coarse and simple beauty is stunning to Thut-nefer, who holds his breath unintentionally, watching her every movement.

"What are you looking at, o' Sesh? Is something wrong?" she asks, noticing him staring at her.

"No . . . nothing."

"Really?"

"Yes, really."

Their eyes meet in the glow of the embers, fire upon fire.

From within their hearts and minds, a fire burns, leaving its everlasting mark.

In the distance, Thut-nefer hears the shuffle of footsteps and the muffled sound of voices being carried by the evening breeze.

Meryt-mi-hapi crouches next to him. In her hand, she menacingly brandishes the crude wooden harpoon, her eyes keen and shining in the dark of the night.

The sound of voices grows louder and louder, occasionally being drowned out by the passing breeze rustling the reeds along the canal.

He signals quietly to Meryt-mi-hapi to fade into the shadows of the dimness, while she hands him the harpoon and vanishes quickly

Thut-nefer sits up and takes a drink from the earthenware jug. The gurgling sound of the cool water as it pours out of the jug into his mouth seems deafening in the silence.

The muscles in his back tense up in anticipation. He holds onto the harpoon firmly, ready to strike if necessary.

A voice calls out a greeting from a short distance away. Thut-nefer recognizes the accent immediately. *But can it be possible?* he wonders.

"Greetings o fisherman! May we approach your humble fire?"

Thut-nefer, unsure, momentarily squints into the darkness towards the approaching figures, waiting for the fire to shed its luminosity upon their faces.

Meryt-mi-hapi, recognizing her brother's voice, steps out from the shadows and stands behind Thut-nefer, waiting for his gesture of welcome.

"Welcome, strangers, to our humble camp in the domain of our Lord of Stretches of Water and Fishes," he grunts, gruffly playing his part as headman.

She rushes towards her brother and embraces him. Nar looks over at Thut-nefer, who sits grinning from ear to ear.

"You almost had me fooled, my noble sesh; but your accent gave you away," he manages to blurt out between embraces.

Thut-nefer looks at the second figure standing aloof, a short distance away, the flickering of the fire reflecting on his clean shaven head.

Ibeby, Priest of Serqet, steps forward, shaking his thick, wooden staff, cut from the holiest of trees, accompanied by the familiar rattle of beads that follow any of his movements.

His pointed nose twitches in excitement, and his eyes glisten with an incandescent light, even in the darkness of the night.

"There you are, my young Sesh, we've been looking for you all day."

"Greetings, o' Priest," Thut-nefer answers respectfully and stands up to welcome him, offering him his place by the fire.

"You're the last person I expected to see tonight. Must be that our fate is interlocked, like two snakes in mortal combat."

"Yes, indeed, ever since the day I met you at the temple of Ptah. I have some news for you and also a letter from your friend, Memi."

He hands him a scroll of papyrus folded neatly, in the manner only used by scribes when passing messages.

Thut-nefer stokes up the fire, adding the last remaining chunks of wood, and begins to unfold the papyrus carefully, enjoying the undoing of each fold in the prescribed manner.

He looks over at Meryt-mi-hapi, happily chattering away with her brother. Her face is beaming with happiness, her eyes shining like a freshly polished piece of carnelian.

"Bring some food and beer, Meryt-mi-hapi! Our guests must be hungry after their long walk."

"Who is a guest of whom?" Nar asks impertinently, a large grin splattered all over his round, tanned face. The trademark blue lotus dangles around his neck, proclaiming him a sailor of the great river.

He grasps his rope and winds it around his shoulder, grabs his pouch and stands up, his short, stocky body swaying gently, as if he had the wooden planks of a vessel under his feet.

"Your wish is my command, o' Scribe of the holy city of Men-nefer!"

They all burst out laughing, thankful that the thread of destiny had brought them all safely back together.

Comfortably nestled by the fire, they begin to exchange stories, sipping at the beer jugs that Memi had sent with Nar for his dear friend in exile.

Ibeby, noticing Thut-nefer's quiet and sombre mood, nudges him with his arm playfully, hoping to distract him from his thoughts.

"Your neighbour has been taken ill, and I have heard that the swnwn treating him has asked for a priest of Serqet to continue with the treatment. I have been notified by my Order to attend to this wretch of a man. It seems he has high connections."

The priest pauses briefly and scratches his clean shaven head, fighting away the mosquitoes pestering him.

"Your heart is pure, dear Sesh, as it seems the man is quite ill. The swnwn has not yet found a cure to his ailment. I can refrain from going altogether, and we can let the poor man suffer in his evil ways. Yet, I am obliged to warn you that if you do, then it will affect you in the long run.

The best medicine to any ailing heart is forgiveness. Forgive and your heart will lighten up like wild quails scattering from the papyrus thickets at the first sense of approaching nets."

Ibeby looks at his friend thoughtfully waiting for his reply.

Nar and Meryt-mi-hapi now being drawn into the conversation look at both the priest and the scribe intently waiting patiently for the heart of the man they both love to proclaim his Maat.

Thut-nefer gazes into the embers of the fire watching the different shades of red interplay together.

He sees, in his mind's eye, the fat nobleman sitting on his chair unabashed, pouring the precious oil of myrrh on his head, while being carried by his half-starved servants, their rib cages clearly protruding through their wrinkled skin.

Thut-nefer then sees the devastated bee hives, scattered all over the ground, and the precious honey gone.

He looks away from the fire in disgust.

"Go to him, o' Priest of Serqet, and heal his ailment."

"Say that with a pure heart, o' Sesh," declares Ibeby with a grimace." "Speak the truth, even if it leads you to your death."

"Yes, I say that with a pure heart. Forgiveness is the best medicine for an ailing heart. Just as Atum loves his creations, I, too, will. Who am I to complain?"

The priest jumps up and kisses Thut-nefer on the shoulders. Nar and Meryt-mi-hapi do likewise.

"Your Maat has spoken with great justice, o' Sesh," Meryt-mi-hapi whispers to him, squeezing his arm tenderly.

Thut-nefer, moved by his companions' heartfelt reaction, wipes his watery eyes inconspicuously.

"When Ra wept, his tears were turned into honey bees. Let your tears fly, so that they may produce honey and sweeten your ailing heart. *That's* forgiveness," Ibeby chants quietly.

A silence settles down upon them as they all look at the wise priest in awe.

Thut-nefer begins to read aloud the note delivered by Ibeby, squinting at the small letters written by Memi's neat handwriting.

"It seems that the governor is desperate. He is going to raze the mud hut down to the ground, in hopes that they will find any evidence of the missing title-deed. Life, health and prosperity, Memi."

*   *   *

The morning mist lays thick on the swampy canal, hugging the water with a steamy embrace.

Thut-nefer opens his eyes, gently allowing the dim first light to play its last nocturnal drama.

The fishing boats glide through the river's mist, like a forlorn soul wandering through a temple in search of his ka.

A lonely voice begins to sing, softly at first, then louder, as the boatman's oars move in unison. The fishermen, returned from their labour at the harvest, slowly release their nets into the waters, happy again to be back among their beloved swamp.

> "For you are started songs with the harp,
> For you they sing with hand-claps,
>
> For you youths and children shout out,
> For you the crowds are assembled.
>
> One who comes with riches, adorning the land,
> one who makes fresh the hue of the bodies of men,
>
> who enlivens the heart of the pregnant woman,
> who loves the multitude of herds.
>
> All people raising the praise of the Ennead
> Have fear for the awe made by his son, the Lord of All, to make the Two Riverbanks verdant
>
> Verdant the spirit at your coming,
> Verdant the spirit at your coming, o' Flood,
> Verdant the spirit at your coming.[109]"

The childlike screeches of a nearby white ibis colony, accompanied by the eerie sound of the fisherman's song, awakens the others. Thut-nefer checks on his friends as they begin to stir.

Totally wrapped up in their linen sheets, like a bunch of mummies waiting to be completed, they are strewn around the campfire, in hope that the rising smoke would deter the marauding mosquitoes and keep them at bay.

---

[109] Hymn to the Flood

He waves off some of the pestering insects buzzing around his ears, while watching Ibeby peer out from under his sheet.

"Good morning," the priest spits out, coughing. He gets up and rolls up his bedding, carefully adjusting his robe and beads.

Thut-nefer looks at Ibeby curiously, examining all of the paraphernalia dangling from around his body and neck.

"Do you ever take off your beads?" he asks the priest cautiously, not wishing to offend him.

"Never," he replies. "The beads are a part of me and I am part of them.

With a vague smile creeping across his thin face, he scoffs, "We compliment one another towards the manifestation of magic. I hope you've been clever enough to keep the frog amulet close."

Thut-nefer searches for his amulet, making sure it is still secure in its place. Satisfied, he places his hand on Ibeby's shoulder in quiet gratitude.

*   *   *

It has been several hours, now, since Nar had left to fetch the tomb-robbers. He knew that they would best know how to circumvent the Governor's men at the mud hut.

It was no easy task to find their whereabouts, but he had been persistent. He knew, only too well, that these men worked under the cover of the night.

Nar had made their acquaintance when they were in hiding and had asked him to supply them with fish and bread.

He had eventually found the three men, sand still plastered all over their faces, carrying their digging utensils, their fingers and nails broken and chafed from the constant digging, their garments in tatters. Nar knew their appearance to be deceptive, just as their ways.

They live among the shadows, he surmised, *loathed by the people. Not daring to show their faces during the day, they seek shelter with the rats. Even the swine-herders trample on them when they find an opportunity, guarding their beasts like hawks.*

Nar walks up to them warily.

"Greetings, o' fisherman! What brings you to us," the elder of the three asks, wiping the sand from his face to reveal a nasty scar running down the side of his cheek.

"When you were hungry, I fed you. Now, I need a small payment in return."

"We have nothing to offer, fisherman. It's been a bad night. Go back and salt your fish," one of them grunts.

He plunges his hands into the irrigation ditch, scoops out a handful of water and splashes his face with it.

"A little of your time will be a form of payment," Nar counters, hoping that they would go for the bait.

The three men look at each other, incredulously, and then back at Nar.

"And what have *you* got to offer?"

"A piece of turquoise, of the highest quality, brought to me by sailors of Henen-nesut.[110]"

The scar on the elderly tomb robber begins to dance on his face, as he breaks into a ruthless smile.

Nar quickly explains to the three men what is required of them.

"Can be done, fisherman, and anyway, we have a score to settle with the Governor and his men," he answers gruffly. "Lead the way."

---

[110]   Henensu: Heracleopolis

Chapter 19

Thut-nefer and Meryt-mi-hapi wave their farewells to Ibeby as he disappears behind the fisherman's encampment, a lone figure walking, shoulders stooping, carrying the burdens of a new day, into the rising sun.

"We must hurry, before Ra shines his blessings," Nar calls out to Thut-nefer breathlessly, several paces ahead of the rugged tomb-robbers, who are scrambling behind.

"They're going to create a diversion and draw out the Governor's thugs, so that you can get inside the hut. I'm going to cover your back, while Meryt-mi-hapi will be by your side. I know her all too well—she'll refuse to stay behind," Nar mumbles earnestly, his voice trembling with excitement.

"Good, good," Thut-nefer answers, trying to keep his own excitement under wraps.

"May Atum have mercy on us and bless our undertakings. O' Sobek, you are the avenger, an offering to you, if you stand by us!" he proclaims stoically, as he watches the tomb-robbers approach the mud hut from the front, vociferously hurling their abusive insults from all sides.

Within moments, Thut-nefer hears the angry voices of the Governor's men respond, as they begin pouring out of the mud hut, sleep still confusing their sense of reality.

Unused to this sort of abuse, their pride ruffled up like the feathers of a quail ready to be plucked. They shout back derisively.

"Now," Thut-nefer whispers hoarsely to his feminine partner in stealth, and they both run for the cover of the palm trees near the hut. Unseen the pair slips through the doorway.

The musty smell of incense greets Thut-nefer's nose, yet the overwhelming stench of unwashed bodies soon blots out the sweet scent.

Meryt-mi-hapi, standing by his side, wields her deadly flint blade, carefully watching the door. Thut-nefer reaches for a stick and breaks open the hole under the beam, in order to retrieve the title-deed.

He quickly camouflages the hole with a piece of palm bark, grabs Meryt-mi-hapi by the waist, and looks around the hut for the last time.

Nar calls quietly through the small window from around the back of the hut.

"Hurry up! The tomb-robbers are beginning to have troubles, and once violence breaks out, they're going to scatter back into the shadows, like the rats they are!"

Once outside, Thut-nefer and Meryt-mi-hapi scuttle for shelter, then slide into an irrigation ditch just high enough to conceal their presence.

Slipping and sliding on their bellies, like grounded eels, they slowly work their way away from the mud hut.

Nar, bringing up the rear, lurks behind with an old wooden harpoon in his hand, holding the ground, while Thut-nefer and Meryt-mi-hapi move further away to safety.

One of the Governor's men, a husky looking thug with a soiled white linen kilt, waves his thick wooden staff threateningly at the retreating tomb-robbers, as they scamper through the muddy fields.

Slowly, upon seeing the ragged bunch disappear in the distance, the Governor's men walk back to the hut, grunting and snorting at each other in frustration, cursing at the unexpected disturbance.

Once inside their mud hut—and not noticing a thing—they collapse into their flimsy beds and resume their weary sleep.

Crouching in the irrigation ditch, Thut-nefer recognizes that a great burden had been removed from his heart, like a sack full of stone chippings being carried away by a stone mason's apprentice.

Getting up and finding himself all covered in mud, he walks back to the canal silently, sits down, and begins to wash up. Once done, he slowly chews on a dry loaf of bread. Nar passes him a piece of hard, salted, white cheese and a cucumber.

He looks up at his friend, thankfully mulling over the now-passed events.

"I couldn't have done this without you, fisherman," he remarks abruptly. "May Atum bless your heart and strengthen you."

Thut-nefer looks around for his rigging, and fishes out a half hin jug of beer. He hands the earthenware jug, still cold from the coolness of the night, to Nar, who eagerly draws the plugging and raises it to his mouth, drinking greedily.

From the corner of his eye, he notices Meryt-mi-hapi bathing in the canal.

Only a master sculptor could capture such a figure, Thut-nefer thinks to himself, gazing with wonder and desire, and give it its full accredited beauty . . . and only from the best of stone.

Nar hands him the jug, his eyes gleaming at Thut-nefer's obvious interest in his sister.

"You two are attracted to each other like red dragonflies to a blue lotus. Perching on top of a blossom, the dragonfly allows the lotus' tantalizing scent to fill its senses and so attract its mate," he snorts unabashedly, staring deep into his eyes.

Thut-nefer, not flinching, looks up toward the sun, hoping to diffuse the situation. Not a cloud is in sight. The bright turquoise sky overrules all colours on the ground, except the shadows caused by the strength of the sun.

Nar, not wishing to push too far, breaks into a smile, causing his chubby oval, deeply suntanned face to be covered in long lines of wrinkles.

"The best thing I like about you, fisherman, is your straightforwardness . . . and your truthfulness. That's very hard to find, in these times. Meryt-mi-hapi has a place in my heart, and I will always keep her safe."

Satisfied with the answer, Nar kisses his friend on the shoulder.

*　　*　　*

"Come, my noble Sesh, get into the boat. We can talk while we fish. Cheese and bread do not satisfy my ferocious appetite. Have you forgotten? You need to keep your word and make an offering to the Lord of Stretches of Water and Fishes."

Once out on the brown waters among the papyrus thickets, Thut-nefer feels the tension in his body slowly easing up. He grabs his line, baits his hook, and lowers it gently into the water, wrapping a little line around his finger.

"I can see you had a good teacher," Nar comments quietly.

"Only the best, after you, of course," Thut-nefer smirches, feeling a nibble on his line.

"I traded most of the festival spices for turquoise and carnelian. I hid them in a safe place; and when we get back; I'll give them to you," Nar sputters urgently, wishing to get business matters straight.

"Good, good. Always knew you were a clever man," Thut-nefer answers, satisfied that Nar had managed the transactions so well.

Changing the subject he asks, "Tell me, what's it like in the southlands?"

Nar stares deep into the brown water and frowns before answering. "The river is strong and wide. Flowing with force and abundance, only a strong wind can push a vessel against the current. I only made it as far as Henen-nesut, House of the royal child . . . twentieth nome."

He pauses for a moment and scratches his forehead roughly, leaving some fish scales dangling precariously. Brushing them aside, he continues "I hope to catch the next trader to the port of the south[111]. The Thebans call it the door to the north."

"Sekhet has favored you," Thut-nefer replies. "Your throw sticks have favored you, Nar. Look! The colour of the water is changing," he adds excitedly noticing the greenish streaks in the hue of the brown water.

The greatest wisdom is to know how to listen to the silence of one's environment, to be able to meditate on the words received, and then being able to act accordingly it suddenly strikes him. *Life is a transitory state, and even trees fall.*

Confounded by his thoughts he watches Nar's agility handling his line and the crude boat simultaneously.

---

[111] In the nome of Abydos

Thut-nefer pulls in his line, finding a small tilapia dangling at the end, unhooks it and throws it into the basket. He drops his line into the water again.

"Yes, Sesh, that's the first sign of the approaching flood. Hope that Atum will bless us with a Great Hapi[112]"

Nar looks up and smiles at the scribe, hunched up in the papyrus skiff, dangling his line over the edge, as if he was just a common fisherman.

"You're a very wise fisherman, o' Scribe of the Holy City of Men-nefer," he comments dryly, stifling an affectionate laugh. Finally, unable to hold back his mirth any longer, he laughs heartily.

Thut-nefer knowing only too well that he is the brunt of Nar's amusement, allows himself a wry smile.

"The deaf man who does not hear is insensitive. And when one is insensitive, communication breaks down. A breakdown in communication can only lead to violence. And violence will only lead to the law of the strong over the weak."

Nar, wide-eyed and no longer laughing, looks at the scribe earnestly.

"You teach me the power of the Great River," Thut-nefer notes, quoting an ancient poem. "And I teach you the power of the Great Symbols. Listen well.

> To whom can I speak today?
> Brothers are evil
> And the friends of today unlovable
>
> To whom can I speak today?
> Hearts are rapacious
> And everyone takes his neighbor's goods.

---

[112]   High inundation.

To whom can I speak today?
Gentleness has perished
And the violent man has come down on everyone.

To whom can I speak today?
Men are contented with evil
And goodness is neglected everywhere.

To whom can I speak today?
He who should enrage a man by his ill deeds,
he makes everyone laugh (by) his wicked wrongdoing.

To whom can I speak today?
Men plunder
And every man robs his neighbor.

To whom can I speak today?
The wrongdoer is an intimate friend
And the brother with whom one used to act is become an
enemy.

To whom can I speak today?
None remember the past
And no one now helps him who used to do good.

To whom can I speak today?
Brothers are evil,
And men have recourse to strangers for affection.

To whom can I speak today?
Faces are averted,
And every man looks askance at his brethren.

To whom can I speak today?

Hearts are rapacious

And there is no man's heart in which one can trust.

To whom can I speak today?[113]"

A cool breeze picks up the last words and rustles them among the reeds and papyrus thickets. A silence engulfs the two men, as they sit opposite one another, staring into the murky, greenish water.

Their companionship had bonded and no amount of words could gratify the silence.

"Thut-nefer . . ."

"Yes, Nar . . . Lost in time . . . he whose name is spoken lives!"

Their eyes meet and silence engulfs them once again. Thut-nefer picks up gently where he had left off.

"To whom can I speak today?

There is no contented man,

And that person who once walked with him no longer exists.

To whom can I speak today?

I am heavy-laden with trouble

Through lack of an intimate friend.

To whom can I speak today?

The wrong which roams the earth,

There is no end to it.[114']

---

[113]   Debate between a man tired of his life and soul. Translated by R.O. Faulkner in W. K. Simpson, ed., *The Literature of Ancient Egypt*, New Haven & London, 1973, pp. 201-209

[114]   Ibid

Thut-nefer pauses for a moment. Catching his breath he looks at his friend, to see if he had lost him in the whirl of the magic of the symbols.

Nar, undeterred, pulls out another tilapia from the greenish brown waters.

"You asked about the southlands?" Nar asks, looking over his shoulder at Thut-nefer. "Well, they have a strong king who frowns upon the rulers of Men-nefer, for their wrongdoings.

His governors are kept in line and no one can go against his will. His Maat is good. He feeds his people and does not overburden them with taxation. Justice prevails and one law applies to all.

That's what I heard from his sailors. They sail the length of the Great River unobstructed, knowing their King stands behind them. They all seem content and trade with them is very beneficial . . ."

"Yes, Nar, indeed," Thut-nefer cuts in, "Atum creates strong rulers to fortify the backbones of the weak and to counteract the blows of fate, unlike our King and his Governor, who walk around in all their pomp.

Meanwhile the multitudes starve, and they grow fatter and fatter. Without Maat, everything is lost."

Nar gazes down at the laden wicker basket nestled between his knees. Satisfied with the catch, he gently manoeuvres the boat through the papyrus thickets to the middle of the widening canal.

"The lotuses are closing," Nar remarks sadly. "It's time we get off the water and clean the fish. Pull in your line, Sesh."

Amidst the last thickets, the boat glides through countless lotus leaves floating on the surface of the water, sucking in the sun's rays.

Nar leans over carefully and collects some half-closed lotus blossoms.

He tosses two flowers into Thut-nefer's lap. He then rips away the wilted blossom from around his neck and ties a fresh one in its place, in the traditional manner of all sailors. He nods at Thut-nefer to do the same.

Thut-nefer opens the half-closed blossoms with his fingers and inhales deeply, allowing the aromatic scent to penetrate into his lungs and flow freely through the rivers of his body. As he does so, he immediately feels relief from all the aches and pains in his heart and body.

He gently ties a lotus around his neck, ready to take on what fate has in store for him.

"Now, you're a man of the Great River," Nar comments, proudly pointing to the blue lotus tied around his friend's neck.

"Remember your lessons well. Throw your offering to the Lord of Stretches of Water and Fishes, the great avenger, and thank him for his trust in you."

Nar picks up the old wooden harpoon and points to a small clearing along the bank.

"Look! There he is, basking in the afternoon sun, watching us all along."

Thut-nefer looks over at the magnificent beast, soaking in Ra's blessings, its beady, green eyes motionless, as if staring into oblivion.

He retrieves two fish from the basket and tosses them into the water close to the bank. The crocodile momentarily lies stock-still, like a rough and unfinished statue waiting for the master craftsman to complete his work.

As the minutes drag by and the river's moist heat bring beads of sweat to the two men's brows, the immobile beast stares into nothingness, where time and space join to form the water of the brown swamp.

With slow deliberation, the crocodile slowly moves its body to and fro in a steady rhythm, like a priestess playing a sistrum, creating a current of animation in its stillness. Then, without a sound, it slides gracefully into the quiet current of the canal.

"He's accepted your offering," Nar whispers with an exhilarated tone. A prickly sensation runs down Thut-nefer's spine.

He looks at Nar, wide-eyed with his own excitement, like the flames of a fire jumping from one piece of wood to the next. The thumping of his heart pops his ears, as he watches the river-gliding beast open its jaws (revealing its shiny, white teeth for an instant), swallow the fish and disappear beneath the murky surface.

A soft breeze rustles the reeds, gently rippling the surface. Then silence.

Both men sit transfixed, unable to move, taking in the seemingly prehistoric magic unfolding before them.

All the elements had seemed to gather together in one moment of time for them, blessed by Atum, to lift their souls to a higher level of being, where goodness reigns and evil is crushed.

A gentle repose engulfs Thut-nefer's heart, leaving him serene, peaceful, calm. For a few long moments, his eyesight becomes crystal clear and remarkably focused; he can see colour, line and texture like never before; and yet the entire riverscape before him seems motionless, like the crocodile earlier lying on its bed of mud. Maat.

Thut-nefer listlessly retrieves the meticulously polished frog amulet from under his belt and grasps it tightly. He then slowly opens his palm, allowing it to reflect the sun's light.

In a flash of enlightened insight, Thut-nefer cognizes the magic of the symbols and the magic of the river swirling together into a unified whole, lifting his senses to a transcendent state, like a master Swnwn concocting a consciousness-raising mixture of herbs.

Thut-nefer closes his eyes, and sails inward:

Sobek . . . Maat . . . Heket.

The avenger will lead us to the feather of the balance, and the feather will lead us to the resurrection. The resurrection of good over evil it is, where Maat is a constant driving force, enabling man and nature to accept one another for their mutual benefit.

Atum gives you eyes to see, gives you ears to hear, gives you a heart to feel and a mind to think . . . all of which to overcome the shadows.

May I plead with all my heart for light.

Give us light to love and love to light; for without light, we have nothing, but a swamp and darkness.

And more, I pray for the lotus to continue to bloom across the land.

The light is quickly fading and the sun is ready to embark upon its journey through the nether world. Thut-nefer comes to, as if out of a daze. He hears Meryt-mi-hapi calling from a short distance away. Standing along the edge of the canal, she waves her arms frantically in the hope of attracting their attention.

His eyes slowly focus on his friend's face, his body sluggish and drained. Akhet, the entrance to the Underworld, beckons to him, momentarily leaving a misty veil in its place.

Without the river we are nothing, he muses shaking his head *Let the evil vanish and spread into thin air, rejoicing at the sound of its hissing, as it is sucked up into Akhet, the points at the horizon where the sun rises every morning and sets every night.*

"Where have we been?" Nar croaks, as he beaches the flimsy craft.

Meryt-mi-hapi comes running and steadies the papyrus skiff, helping to pull it up onto the bank.

"You've been gone for a long time. Was the fishing good?"

As Nar hands her the basket with the catch, she expertly balances it on her head.

"You're both so quiet, I've been so busy helping our hosts with their chores. The headman is back from the city and is looking forward to meeting you. He has ordered a feast in your honour, o Sesh!" she exclaims proudly, looking at Thut-nefer with her sensuous black eyes.

"Come now," she orders, eagerly grabbing both men by their arms, the basket still meticulously perched on her head.

*   *   *

Chapter 20

Thut-nefer sits by the crackling fire, watching the old fisherman expertly turn the staked tilapia from side to side. His blistered hands are like untreated hide: calloused and darkly spotted where constant blisters had opened and healed, opened and healed.

The old man's face is deeply tanned. The glare of the sun's reflection off the water had taken its toll. Wrinkles, like a river branching out into the delta, flow down along the sides of his eyes.

Slightly paler, and obviously derived from constant squinting the pale lines give him a fierce look. Nestled deep in his tan his black eyes twinkle with a shine of life's ecstasy.

He stokes the fire with a stick causing the embers to glow and the fish to sizzle softly in the quiet of the evening.

"I've heard many good things about you, o' Scribe. Your Ba is gentle and you haven't forgotten your Maat."

Thut-nefer looks at the man intently watching his every movement. His eyes are glued to the fish on the fire, his every movement pointing to his expertise in grilling.

"A man with no Maat is like a tomb robber with no tomb to rob; even without evil deeds, his is the disgrace."

Thut-nefer nods his head humbly, in awe of this simple man.

Meryt-mi-hapi approaches and lays bread, onions and cucumbers on the reed mat next to the old fisherman. He gently nods his head in gratitude, while watching her feline figure turn gracefully.

"She is a good girl, obedient; yet she has a tongue as sharp as any gutting knife," he notes, breaking into a smile. "Just like her mother. You know, good Sesh, we're all inter-related, through our women, like a net," he laughs gruffly.

"Once you get caught, then you naturally become part of the mesh."

He lets his own tongue wander over his cracked parched lips, allowing the moisture to alleviate the dryness.

"When her father died," he adds solemnly, "he made me take an oath out on the river that I would watch out for her."

Nar sits down next to Thut-nefer and hands the old fisherman a hin jug of beer. The man delicately raises the earthenware jug to his lips and slowly drinks, savoring every drop.

For the first time that evening, he looks at both of them, a bright twinkle in his eyes, like Sopdet [115] rising above the horizon declaring the arrival of a new year.

He smiles wryly, and then wipes away the beer from the corners of his mouth with the back of his hand.

"I gather you boys had an encounter with He Who Keeps The Energies Together[116]. I can tell by the ridiculous look on your faces!"

---

[115] Sirius

[116] Nehebu-Kau

He laughs heartily. The sound coming from the depths of his heart reverberates through Thut-nefer's own heart, like a timeless echo resounding in the inner sanctuary of his tomb.

"The first encounter is always like that," declares the old man forcefully. "How many fish did you land with this afternoon? It was seven, no doubt."

He pauses for a moment, again lifting the jug of beer to his lips and drinking unhurriedly. He signals to Nar to turn the stakes of fish, while he stokes the fire.

"Neheb-Kau assembles all the different energies of the universe together, like all the rivers in your body flowing to your heart, causing a totality of one energy ready to burst into one vast illumination."

The coals in the fire burn intensely, creating a luminous and eerie glow on the old fisherman's face.

"He is indestructible and an invulnerable snake. Only Atum can control his vast power, by pressing his nail into his spine. One source of his power, as the ancient story goes, is that he swallowed seven cobras, causing the number seven to be magical."

The moon, red as the embers of their fire, slowly works its way up its destined path across the sky, patiently illuminating the atmosphere. Thut-nefer, captivated by the wonders of Atum's creation unfolding before him, gives little thought to anything else.

Somewhere in the distance of his mind he hears the old fisherman . . . "He Who Harnesses The Spirits is the son of Serqet, our protector here and in the underworld. May Atum have mercy on us."

Meryt-mi-hapi, standing nearby with a look of dismay on her face, breaks the silence.

"While you were out on the water, I walked over to your mud hut, o' Sesh. I'm sorry to say, they have destroyed it completely, leaving no mud brick standing. Your possessions are strewn all over the ground."

She looks at Thut-nefer with a sadness creeping into her eyes. Her indomitable spirit quickly repulses the sadness, however, and her eyes begin to shine with brightness.

"Do not overly grieve at a loss and be not overjoyed when something is given to you," she advises flatly, her natural woman's practicality taking the better of her.

I can feel your presence, o' Ibeby, Thut-nefer thinks to himself. *Have you conjured Nehebu-Kau, son of Serqet, to protect us from our own foolhardiness? Yes, He who harnesses the spirits is our invisible protector and only with Atum's permission.*

The old cattle herder comes to his mind, the rugged, leathery face clearly dancing before him. He recalled the old man had once told him to cry to Atum with all his heart, like a lost calf crying for its mother.

Thut-nefer gazes up at the sky. Moonlight has taken precedence over all else, leaving the night sky devoid of its stars.

"O Atum, give us light, as Ra has given light to the moon," Thut-nefer cries out loud with all his heart. Facing great injustice is painful, but he longs even more to have his connection to Atum sustained.

Only through such a sustenance can he reach Maat. For Maat has to unfold like a bird stretching its wings. One feather next to the other, tightly knit together to be able to capture the flow of the wind.

Nar squeezes his friend's arm in compassion, hoping to steady him.

"Well said, o Sesh! May Atum give you the strength to uphold your Maat," the old fisherman proclaims ecstatically.

"And now let us form a circle and all eat together," he adds jovially, "after all, aren't we all creations under the sun? Even the ants will have their share!"

The old man splits a loaf of bread into two and hands Thut-nefer a half. A few crumbs fall to the ground.

*   *   *

The journey back home has been long, but Thut-nefer is not tired. A sense of freshness of soul has engulfed him. The last days have taught him much, giving him a new sense of triumph over the intricacies of the human swamp.

Thut-nefer walks proudly, his scribe utensil's basket dangling from his shoulder and his wig firmly placed on his head.

In his right hand, his Was sceptre is thrust out forward, as though leading the line. Meryt-mi-hapi and Nar bring up the rear, as is customary, blending in with the traffic of human bodies circulating about.

A barber sitting on a wooden stool at the corner, patiently waiting for customers, polishes his bronze instruments to a shine. He looks up at the scribe and his small entourage, greets him humbly, and offers his services.

Thut-nefer nods to him and the man quickly closes his wooden box and falls in behind Meryt-mi-hapi, happy at last to have found some work.

A beggar, flies glued around his eyes, accosts Thut-nefer waving his empty earthenware bowl with a starkness rarely seen.

Nar steps up and harshly shoos the man away, dislodging the swarm of flies from around his eyes into a wispy black cloud.

"What is this city turning into," he shouts at the retreating beggar.

The man immediately threatens Nar by raising his food bowl in defiance, countering, "Go back to the swamp, you river rat!"

Nar loses his patience and lunges forward, in a crude attempt to grab the vagabond.

Thut-nefer reaches back and grabs hold of his friend by the arm, restraining him with all his might. The young fisherman pulls at Thut-nefer's strong grasp, like a hooked eel slashing from left to right.

"Let him go, Nar! He's a poor, filthy wretch, and it's a sign of the times. Hunger and humility do not go hand in hand."

He watches as Nar settles down and feels his muscles relax; in turn, Thut-nefer eases his grip. The donkey feeling the line go lax pulls hard, only knowing too well that it is close to home.

Meryt-mi-hapi, balancing the wicker basket on her head, tries to restrain it. A moment later, the line breaks and the donkey scurries away, only to stop to chew on a nearby patch of trampled weeds.

The beggar, now a short distance away, throws his cracked bowl at Nar in a flurry of disgraced anger. His humiliation is apparent on the smiles of passersby, who slow down to watch the incident.

The bowl hits Meryt-mi-hapi's basket, ricocheting off and striking the unsuspecting barber on his head with a thud. He groans in anguish and collapses, a small pool of blood forming on the dusty path beneath him.

Meryt-mi-hapi kneels next to the barber and raises his torso onto her knees. The man groggily comes to, and she applies a piece of linen to his wound, which stops the bleeding.

He looks up at her thankfully and mumbles incoherently, obviously still in a daze.

"My wooden work-box, my tools . . ." he manages to croak looking around in despair.

A crowd had now formed, beginning to chant for justice. Thut-nefer, no longer able to restrain Nar, lets him go after the beggar.

Three men hold the quivering beggar in front of Thut-nefer. The flies have abandoned him, leaving his destitute eyes plainly visible.

"Throw him to the crocodiles!" shouts one man.

Nar brings down his fist heavily into the beggar's back, causing him to stumble and then fall onto his knees.

Thut-nefer raises his Was Sceptre into the air demanding calm.

"Whatever the eyes see," he declares, "the ears hear, and the nose breathes goes straight to the heart, and the conclusion reached by the heart is then spoken by the tongue."

Two burly thugs break through the crowd, brandishing their thick wooden staffs, demanding to know what the commotion is all about.

One of the men strikes the kneeling beggar viciously, knocking him out cold. The crowd, taken aback by the brutality, falls silent.

No one wishes to give testimony.

Afraid of purely sadistic violence, the group of people gathered around begins to disperse quietly, preferring to watch from a safer distance.

Thut-nefer steps up in front of the beaten beggar, laying unconscious in the dust.

"This man shall be taken to the higher Administrative court for justice, as blood has been spilled," Thut-nefer warns the two burly men.

"Move aside! This man shall be beaten until he is no more," the leader retaliates, bearing his broken front teeth in a display of fierceness, like a wild baboon.

Thut-nefer thumps his Was sceptre hard on the ground with unflinching resolve.

"I am a scribe of this Holy City of Men-nefer and this wretch shall be brought to justice at the King's administrative court," he bellows above the din of the bystanders.

The two rough men move forward, closing in on Thut-nefer, disregarding all that has transpired, grunting disrespectfully.

Thut-nefer stands his ground. Behind him, Meryt-mi-hapi and Nar close ranks. The wounded barber stands up painfully in solidarity with the group and leans against Nar.

More and more bystanders begin to fall in behind the courageous scribe, who has single-handedly defied the governor's brutal men in the hope of allowing justice to prevail.

Somewhere dormant in that day's darkness, the young lotus bud has fought its way up against the current to break through the surface and shine its tender, yet brilliant light.

While the scribe breathes deeply, his thoughts turn to his true source. *The sharper the light, the closer you are to your Maat.*

Suddenly, the ugly man with the broken teeth strikes.

Thut-nefer feels the excruciating pain rampage through his body, as the ruffian's thick staff hits him on the shoulder. His ear throbs.

"To say! To say!" he shouts, burying his pain in the loudness and intensity of his voice, mesmerizing all those around him.

"The knife which castrates! Brilliant, brilliant; triumphant, triumphant. Let the seaman cast off his garments, as a sail for the boat of the sun![117]"

With fury, Thut-nefer rams his sceptre, shaped like a delicate young lotus leaf still waiting to unravel itself, straight into the man's mouth, shattering what few teeth he had left.

Thut-nefer shouts again at the bewildered thug, as the man groans uncontrollably, spitting out his blood and broken teeth onto the dusty path.

"To say! Face falls on face; face sees face. A knife, coloured black and green, goes out against it, until it has swallowed that which it has licked![118]"

Nar and Meryt-mi-hapi stand by close, watching every movement of the brute, in anticipation of any possible retaliatory blow, for they can see the malicious look germinating in his hateful dark eyes.

Thut-nefer turns around, away from the man, raising his sceptre above his head and facing the crowd that had formed behind him.

"I am a listener who listens to the truth, who ponders it in the heart . . . straight and true like Thoth," he exclaims with pride.

Standing tall, he waves his sceptre again above his head, desperately trying to conceal the pain in his shoulder.

The unthinkable has happened. A scribe violated in public by some scruffy hoodlums, who know nothing but the use of violence, in blind support of their master.

The crowd begins to chant in unison.

"Man of justice before the two lands! Man of justice before the two lands!"

---

[117] Utterance 377 of the Pyramids Texts. Translated by Mercer.
[118] Utterance 229 of the Pyramids Texts. Translated by Mercer.

They were now ready to lay down their lives in the protection of their scribe.

Smelling the sweet breath of the north wind playing across his cheeks, Thut-nefer again raises his voice above the chants of the throng, reminding them of the words of the ancients.

"The fire is laid, the fire shines, the incense is placed on the fire, and the incense shines![119]"

The angry crowd begins to move in, slowly encircling the governor's men, like a snake tightening its grip on its prey before it unleashes its fatal bite.

Fearing for their lives, the thugs retreat, pushing their way through the intensifying mob.

Nar pulls at Thut-nefer's arm, jerking him roughly, breaking the flow of adrenalin pumping through his veins.

"Quick, Sesh, we must get you out of here," he whispers urgently in his ear.

Meryt-mi-hapi, standing closely behind, pulls at the donkey moving forward, so as to break open a path through the crowd, like their old fishing boat forcing its way through the reeds.

The barber holds onto the donkey's rig, and he stumbles forward, still in a stunned and bloody daze.

"Take care of that beggar until he comes to, and move him somewhere else before the governor's men come back in force," Thut-nefer orders a few of the bystanders.

"We will, o' scribe! You get a move on!"

Thut-nefer looks around at the faces of his people, both young and old. They all have one thing in common: a deep longing for justice, in a land where Maat no longer prevails. This one sentiment pours out of their hearts, like water being decanted over sacred words in a spouted dish.

---

[119] Utterance 269 Unas pyramid texts

Raising his arms above his head, he cajoles his life force to the fore and lifts his eyes to the sky silently praying: *Ammit, Devourer of the Dead, Great of Death, annihilator of the criminal souls of men, rid us of them, so we may live in peace.*

A young priest, observing Thut-nefer from afar, calls out to the scribe with compassion, "A cry for the wind of justice can only be caught in the wings of the great bird hovering high in the sky bathing in the light of Ra."

An Ankh and two raised arms[120] flash through Thut-nefer's mind like a kingfisher diving for its prey. The magic of the symbols wrestle their way out of his subconscious causing him to falter briefly.

He shakes off his vacillation, feeling his life force integrate with his actions.

Thut-nefer turns towards the stranger and smiles. "The spouted dish is carved from a single piece of stone so that it can absorb the powers of its inscriptions," he calls back, as he resists Nar's frantic yanking at his arm, trying to pull him towards the gap in the crowd.

*   *   *

---

[120]   Ankh and two raised arms are the hieroglyphic symbol for life force

Chapter 21

Thut-nefer's family's errand boy opens the creaky old door and peers out from behind it. In his hand, he holds a piece of palm string attached to the neck of a chameleon. His eyes flicker back and forth, like the curious creature being dragged along by the boy.

Thut-nefer enters first, but allows Nar and the barber to pass. He pulls Meryt-mi-hapi by the arm and whispers to her urgently before the household learns of their arrival.

"Take the title deed, wrap it up in some used cloth, and bury it deep in the silo!"

He watches her as she turns, flicks off her sandals, and runs agilely towards the silos, weaving through the fast approaching members of the household, finally disappearing behind a row of lemon trees.

"The master is back! Our Sesh is back!" voices shout across the courtyard.

The overseer comes running, dropping a basket full of wheat he has just finished chaffing in the wind. Holding the wooden spade tightly, he comes to an abrupt halt. Thut-nefer notices he has neatly fitted the tail skin of a cow on the handle, allowing it a good grip.

"Greetings, o' Sesh," he proclaims respectfully, his kind eyes dancing with excitement at the sight of his beloved master.

"Greetings, Overseer," Thut-nefer replies, equally happy to see the caretaker of his family's lands.

"Take care of the barber. He's been wounded, and send for the Swnswn."

Having barely finished the sentence, the piercing loud shrieks of women in distress can be heard at the door.

The overseer and Nar bolt towards the door, with Thut-nefer not far behind. He feels a little stiff, his shoulder still throbbing from the blow he had received. Yet the high pitched shrieks had shocked him into action, making him forget his own pain.

Nar lifts a young girl into his arms, wiping the blood from her face with his forearm.

Perplexed, Thut-nefer looks around. Seeing no evidence of any violent perpetrators, his eyes venture towards the shrieking women huddled together in fear. Their white linen dresses are stained red and jaggedly torn.

The overseer shoves Thut-nefer hard and he stumbles, his foot slipping out of his sandal, causing him to fall heavily against the wall and then to the ground. He coughs out dust and clears his nostrils, rubbing his eyes.

There stands a lean jackal, poised ready to kill. Facing the overseer and growling fiercely, its protruding white fangs curve inwards shining through its dark lips, dripping red with blood

Its beady black eyes shine fearlessly in the face of danger, as it stares down its next victim.

The overseer threatens it with his wooden spade, in the vain hope of scaring it off. The beast only growls more viciously.

Thut-nefer slowly reaches for his Was scepter laying on the ground next to his feet. The animal's low, heavy rolling sound signals his readiness to pounce and tear to shreds any one wishing to get in its way.

"Wepwawet, opener of the ways, face your death or retreat!" Thut-nefer shouts to the growling animal, watching the golden-gray fur standing up erect from around its neck.

"Lead us through the underworld in peace, o' Opener of the Ways! You've caused enough harm here, be on your way! Release the anger in your heart, for it only attracts more anger . . . and more anger attracts more evil!"

He pauses briefly, and looks into the darkly lit eyes of the snarling canine before him.

"I will light some incense for you and let the smoke whirl you through the depths of your heart, subduing the intricacies that have entangled your righteousness of opening the ways."

Thut-nefer still seated in the dust, unable to move, with his back to the wall, stares intently at the wild jackal, waiting for its next move.

"We have all lost our Maat. Man against nature and nature against Man. Where will this lead us? A free for all, an implosion, and a drop into the void. A downward spiral, where the laws of nature are disregarded for the benefit of the accumulation of wealth."

As the jackal rears up and begins to coil the springs of its hind legs, Thut-nefer raises his voice, and intensifies his tone, channeling his entire being into his words.

"Open your mouth, we are told, and we do, to receive the bitter seeds that have dried in our despair, to conquer what is not ours!"

He pushes his back firmly against the wall and stops.

"Wealth lies not in how much land or how many donkeys one possesses, but in the richness of Maat, and how wisely we utilize what we have to help nature follow its course. So be it, o' Opener of the Ways, love your Maat and leave man entangled in his own web, for even the spider will only eat what it needs. Be off, for you have opened our way."

The fiercely postured jackal sways its body from left to right, its shoulder muscles twitching . . . and like a flash of lightning, it bolts towards the west, land of Deshret.[121]

Meryt-mi-Hapi kneels down next to Thut-nefer, looking at him with great respect and concern.

All eyes, actually, look at him. No one speaks. Nar holds the young girl in his arms, comforting her. Only her whimpers can be heard above the north wind. Even the shrieking women huddled together sit in silence, pondering their miraculous rescue.

He nudges Meryt-mi-hapi gently. "Bring me some coals, I will light some incense."

Thut-nefer fishes out a small linen pouch from under his belt. The frog amulet falls to the ground. He picks it up and carefully polishes it, returning the faience its natural shine.

He then places it comfortably on the palm of his hand, as if it is sitting on a large lotus leaf in the middle of a pond, soaking in the last of the sun's rays.

"Scream and rave to your heart's desire," he remarks aloud to all. "Even the baboons are consummated by the sun's fire, for without blessings nothing will grow."

Thut-nefer drops a few balls of the precious incense into the clay brazier handed to him by Meryt-mi-hapi. He feels her soft touch, as she kneels down next to him, giving him a sense of comfort and strength.

Waiting for the ecstasy of the myrrh to erupt, he looks towards the west. The sun glows deeply, spreading a carpet of blood red clouds across the horizon.

---

[121]   Red lands i.e. the desert

"Death is in my sight today," he intones, "as when a sick man becomes well, like going out-of-doors after detention.

Death is in my sight today, like the smell of myrrh, like sitting under an awning on a windy day.

Death is in my sight today, like the perfume of lotuses, like sitting on the shore of the Land of Drunkenness.

Death is in my sight today, like a trodden way, as when a man returns home from an expedition.

Death is in my sight today, as when a man desires to see home, When he has spent many years in captivity[122]

This is for you, o' Wepwawet, opener of the ways!"

*   *   *

Meryt-ra looks at her son with horror. All around her lay the wounded, those bloodied and in frightened shock from the jackal's attack. The swnswn and his apprentice hover over them, carefully bandaging their wounds.

Thut-nefer pops a morsel of bread into his mouth and drinks deeply from the earthenware jar, its cool liquid calming the ache in his throat. He passes the beer jar to Nar with a smile, who winks back with appreciation.

"Greetings, o' Sesh!" Memi shouts from afar, waving his Was sceptre in the air with delight.

"The boy told me you're back. Looks like you've been traveling on the way of Horus[123] and come across some bandits."

---

[122] Translated by R.O. Faulkner
in W. K. Simpson, ed., *The Literature of Ancient Egypt*, New Haven & London, 1973, pp. 201-209

[123] Road to the Sinai

Spotting Meryt-ra, he quickly greets her politely in the traditional manner.

"No such luck, Memi," Thut-nefer answers. "Just Wepwawet!"

"It's the last five days of the year and I haven't had the chance to give him his amulets, yet. I think he has offended Sekhmet in his unruly ways," Meryt-ra ventures.

She hands Memi a few strips of linen cloth.

"Now, recite something from the Book of the Last Day of the Year over those pieces of cloth and tie them around your necks, all of you. It's a dangerous time until Wep Ronpet.[124]"

Memi reaches over and takes the strips of linen from the mistress of the house, settles down next to his friend, and begins reciting:

"A serpent is entwined by a serpent,

when a young hippopotamus coming on the pasture is entwined.

Earth, swallow that which came out of you!

Monster, lie down, glide away![125]"

Allowing the words to swirl over the strips of cloth, now held tightly in his hand, he decides to blow on them seven times as an extra precaution.

Thut-nefer nurses his shoulder, moving his arm in various directions hoping to determine where it hurt the most.

"Doer, doer, passer-by, passer-by, May thy face look backward! Beware of the Great Door![126]" he mutters to himself, aware of the stress and anxiety the last five days of the year bring to everyone who anticipates the coming flood.

---

[124] First day of the New Year.

[125] Utterance 225 Unas Pyramid texts

[126] Utterance280 Ibid

The Swnswn begins his examination and pokes Thut-nefer's shoulder gently, searching for any cracks in the bones. Satisfied there are no broken bones, he rubs in a concoction to help with the swelling.

Calm finally descends on the household, and even the wounded feel somewhat at ease.

Soon, all are conscious, it would be the going forth of Sepdet[127] and a new hope. The old year would extinguish itself in the black mud of the incoming flood, and the New Year would be born with the light of Sopdet, as it rises from the umduat.

Meryt-mi-hapi stands by Meryt-ra, glancing furtively at Thut-nefer from the corner of her eye.

"Don't bury your heart in unnecessary evil," the mistress of the house proclaims breathlessly, while neatly arranging figs on the large faience plate, so as to compliment the evening meal.

"For, who knows what is hidden in the shades of colours of this magic star, heralding in good or bad news of the incoming flood."

Memi hands Thut-nefer a piece of linen cloth and keeps one for himself, while handing back the rest to Meryt-ra. His gaze falls on Nar, sitting quietly, the young girl still nestled in his powerful arms.

"That's quite unusual for Nar to be sitting alone like that," he comments, turning around and facing Thut-nefer squarely.

Thut-nefer, unfazed, looks Memi straight in the eye.

"Yes, but we had a strange and powerful encounter with He Who Keeps The Energies Together."

Memi lifts both eyelids, allowing his eyeballs to dance in awe. He falls silent for a moment, contemplating the vastness of the universe.

---

[127]   Heliacal rising of Sirius and following it the arrival of the flood

"Received a message from Khentiki," gasps Memi coming to from his reverie, "addressed to the both of us. It seems he is not at all well."

He hands the folded sheet of papyrus to Thut-nefer.

"Oh yes?" Thut-nefer looks at Memi sadly, thinking of his tutor.

The Swnswn sits down on the neatly woven reed mat next to the scribes.

"Our head Swnswn has been treating him lately, and it appears to be his last days," he adds gently.

Thut-nefer nods to Meryt-mi-hapi to bring the evening meal, as he picks up the papyrus and unfolds it carefully. He reads to himself:

"I am meditating on the things that have happened, the events that have occurred in the land. Transformations go on. It is not like last year. One year is more burdensome than the next.

Righteousness is cast out, and iniquity is in the midst of the council hall. The plans of the god are violated, and their dispositions are disregarded. The land is in distress, mourning is in every place, towns and districts are in lamentation. All men alike are under wrongs. As for respect, an end is made of it.

I am distressed because of my heart. It is suffering to hold my peace concerning it. Another heart would bow down, but a brave heart in distress is the companion of its lord.

Would that I had a heart able to suffer. Then would I rest in it. I would load it with words of hope and peace, that I might dislodge through it my malady.

Come then my heart, that I may speak to thee and that thou mayest answer for me my sayings and mayest explain to me that which is in the land.

I am meditating on what has happened.[128]"

---

[128]   The admonitions of Khekheperre-sonbu

Thut-nefer refolds the papyrus and looks up at Memi.

He feels a lifeless ache gnawing at his heart, and it drags him down into his own depths. Thut-nefer allows himself to feel the pain of his mentor's final struggle, wishing he could hold his gaze once more and convey his gratitude for all the wisdom he'd received.

Suddenly, Thut-nefer hears the familiar jingle of beads and shells, bringing with them both light and comfort to the scribe.

As welcome as the sun in a stormy sky, there stands Ibeby, priest of Serqet, in all his raiment, grinning from ear-to-ear, his pointed nose twitching and his freshly shaven head shining.

"Spitting of the wall; vomiting of the brick, that which comes out of thy mouth is thrown back against thyself,[129]" he intones with his familiar demeanor. "Happy to see you, my friend!"

"And me you, Honorable Priest of Serqet," Thut-nefer retorts cheekily. "You always show up unexpectedly, like a scorpion appearing out of nowhere."

They all burst out with laughter that resonates around the courtyard, bringing a smile to all of their once-gloomy faces.

"It seems to me that Maat has left you all stranded . . . but Maat does not exist by itself, without effort.

A continuous counter effort has to be made, to uphold it, and preserve it, against the turbulent forces trying to cause its imbalance," Ibeby warns, no longer smiling, as he, leans against his old wooden staff watching his friends' faces with dismay.

"I have worn a hole in these reed sandals of mine, and it is high time I procure a new pair." He turns to the houseboy." Boy, where is the nearest sandal-maker? Go and fetch me the cheapest pair you can find, so that I may feel the earth between my toes! Walk, walk, walk! That's what I seem to be doing most; yet without walking, I would not get anywhere."

---

[129] *Utterance 229.* Ibid

"Fetch him some sandals, boy," Thut-nefer orders, "at my expense."

"That is most kind of you, scribe of Scribes. Let us walk together barefoot, let us wash in water from the Nile flood, cleanse our ears and mouth with natron. Dress in new clothes and white sandals anointed with perfumed oils and carry an incense burner that we may meet our Maat."

"Indeed, my noble Priest of Serqet, you are always so right."

"We must fight for our Maat," Ibeby declares for all to hear, "each one for his own, and only listen to one's heart. That's why they call me the rogue priest; because I don't listen to anyone."

"They're afraid of your poison," Nar interjects coldly, finally breaking his silence. "Like a delicious looking fish that you eat, but is actually venomous once you've digested it."

A great grin appears on the priest's face, causing the wrinkles around his eyes to dance.

"Fisherman, or is it sailor?" Ibeby smiles, his nose twitching again beyond his control. "Your simple wisdom is well taken! No doubt you have a wise teacher . . ."

"Leave him be, Priest. He means no offence. His tongue is attached to his heart," Thut-nefer intervenes quickly, just moments before Ibeby casts his net.

The venom leaves the priest's eyes and a smile creeps across his face once again.

"Let us eat, I'm starving," Memi blurts out. "The mistress of the house has prepared us a meal. That is a great honour. Sheshu, have the boy bring us some jugs of beer, that we may wash away the remnants of this year!"

He hungrily tears a loaf of bread into two and hands Thut-nefer one half.

* * *

Chapter 22

"Yes, indeed. Is this really the temple of Ptah?" Hussein asks his friend and companion, trudging along the muddy track. He carefully evades a pile of rubbish, holding his breath at the stench.

"Yes, the Temple of Truth," Yussef answers, looking dismally at the broken down granite columns, which lay half-buried in a small lake of fetid sewage water in what is now modern day Memphis.

"So, this is the truth then," replies Hussein, "the truth of our times. The fetid swamp has engulfed us, leaving this once majestic temple rotting. And we are rotting with it! I wonder what it looked like in those days. I bet it was a spectacular piece of architecture, judging by the size of those columns."

Hussein looks gloomily at the encroaching, red brick houses. The rubbish heaps are covered with swarms of flies, looking like an imaginary black blanket spread across the temple and its environs.

And yet the young children play, oblivious to anything but their games.

A dark, musty man approaches the two men, his head wrapped in a dirty woolen scarf. Only his black eyes peer out, and his long, stained robe flashes, as he waves his thick stick.

"Forbidden here," he calls out gruffly in a deep authoritarian voice.

"Do you have any lotus seeds left?" Yussef inquires of Hussein, totally ignoring the guard.

"I have the last two," his friend answers quietly, handing them to him discreetly.

"Forbidden here," the man repeats again.

Yussef tosses the two seeds into the fetid lake and confronts the man.

"Why forbidden?"

"Forbidden here," the man counters, his voice reaching a higher pitch of intensity, like the flies buzzing around him.

Hussein feels faint, as the strong Egyptian sun is taking its toll. Desperately, he looks around for shade, but finds none.

A burning sensation on his head makes him look up briefly. The sun's brightness blurs his vision, but still, through his mind's eye, he can clearly see a frog daintily perched on the prow of the nether bark, guiding it through the darkness.

"Pray that the lotus blooms across the land," Yussef calls out, standing his ground, waiting for the guard to make his move.

The watchman moves in, threatening him with his staff. Hussein pulls Yussef by the shoulder. "Let's go back to my place, before things get nasty."

"Hold on, Hussein. Let's try giving this man some money. Do you have any change?"

"Let it be, Yussef. I don't like the look on his face, plus the stench is getting to me."

"Corruption is stamped all over him," Yussef retorts grimacing. "Do you remember what we read earlier, at your place, from that old book?"

Yussef discreetly slips the guard a crisp five-pound note. The man quickly pockets the note and smiles half-heartedly brushing aside the pestering flies.

"To say: The door of heaven is open, the door of earth is open," Hussein recites, scratching his head trying to recall the remaining text,

"Apertures of the heavenly windows are open,
the steps of Nun are open,
the steps of light are revealed
by that one who endures always
I say this to myself when I ascend to heaven,
that I may anoint myself with the best ointment and clothe myself with
the best linen, and seat myself upon the throne of Truth which makes alive.[130]"

* * *

Sitting on a stone bench by the lotus pond in his garden, one he had so meticulously built, Hussein reflects. The aroma of the lotus blossoms inspires in him a sense of well-being. He gazes up into the sky.

The papyrus plants gently sway in the morning breeze. A kingfisher is perched on a tall papyrus stalk, staring down at Hussein. The large bird proudly bears a white patch on its chest.

Hussein takes a sip of his morning coffee, and watches the red dragonflies fly past his head. He thinks to himself, *It is a miracle and a blessing how we managed to find the seeds and grow this lotus garden.*

---

[130]   Pyramid text: utterance 503. Translation by Mercer.

He recounts in his mind how he and Yussef had bribed an employee at the seed bank to obtain some lotus seeds, after having been turned down by various civil servants.

The bribe to him meant little—it being only a small sum of money—but obviously it was sufficient for the young worker at the seed bank.

Hussein closes his eyes briefly and reflects further. *That was just the beginning of the end . . . or was that the end of the beginning. Who knows where we stand in time?*

Opening his eyes, he stares at the blue lotus floating peacefully on its bed of water, beckoning him gently to follow its path through the haze of time.

Bursting open like a time capsule, the imaginary seed pod scatters its seeds within his mind and soul. He hears words echoing of an age and people he never knew, pleading him to awaken.

Our head is in ancient Memphis and our tail is in the here and now. The snake-that-swallows-its-tail.

And Maat, rushing headfirst through time, waiting for us to pick up the lost threads . . . and proudly stand up to declare to the universe,

"*I uphold Maat!*"

*   *   *

Acknowledgement

Deep gratitude to Willy Mathes for editing my work somewhere in the hills of Alabama while I write at the foot of the step—pyramid. Sakkara, Egypt.

*   *   *

Also, special thanks to Sherif el-Hakim for his wonderful encouragement. For a very brief moment in time we travelled together through time and space.

*   *   *

Milk from the sacred sycamore

I suckle your breast like a fruit
Your heart speaks
I am stronger than you think
This ancient magic tree you thought to be burnt to the roots
Still has magic shoots
Sweet fruits

Sherif el-Hakim

*   *   *